I0739220

Embellish:
Brave Little Tailor Retold

DEMELZA CARLTON

A tale in the Romance a Medieval Fairy Tale series

Copyright © 2017 Demelza Carlton

Lost Plot Press

ISBN- 978-0-9922693-5-7

ISBN-10: 0-9922693-5-0

DEDICATION

This book is for Emmo, who truly appreciates the
value of a well-told tale.
Especially one with dragons..

One

The one thing George loved most in all the world was dragons. At least, he had until a few minutes ago, when the biggest, grumpiest dragon to ever crawl out of a cave had disarmed him and knocked him down with a single swipe of its mighty tail. Now he didn't feel particularly fond of dragons at all.

George raised his head slightly, wondering why he wasn't dead like the charred, armoured corpse beside him. Perhaps the dragon's eyesight was so bad that he thought George was already dead. As soon as George moved, though, the dragon would realise its mistake. And rectify it.

George suppressed a sigh. He didn't lack for courage – he'd challenged the dragon, after all, and he intended to defeat it. But standing before a dragon while the damn dragon held his sword under one claw would only turn him into a piece of toast before the fire, for in one gout of flame, he would be dead, George had no doubt.

Cowardice wasn't his problem. It was common sense, and the ability to see consequences no one else could. The other boys in town would boast of how long other knights had stood while the dragon roasted them with its fiery breath, but George had little admiration for such men. There was honour in defeat if you learned enough from it to ensure victory in the future. What honour was there in taking ten seconds to burn to death before your armour collapsed with your charred bones inside? Even George didn't remember the name of the knight whose body lay beside him. A century from now, no one else would remember him, either. But they would remember the man who slayed the dragon. Even if George wasn't the man to do it today.

The dragon headed down the hill toward the river, distracted by something more interesting than the boy whose sword he'd stolen. George recognised opportunity when he saw it. He leaped to his feet, and sprinted toward the city gates.

His heart hammered in his chest, but he didn't dare stop to look back. All he could focus on was his booted feet pounding the road ever upwards to the safety of the city walls. Fifty yards more. No, forty. Thirty. Twenty-five. Twenty. Fifteen. Ten.

Eight, seven, six…

His fleet feet ate up the distance faster than he stuffed down dumplings at the dinner table.

Three, two, one…

SAFE.

Laughter and applause greeted George as he slowed to enter the city gates.

"Dragon too big for you, boy?"

"No one ever wrote a ballad about a hero running away from a dragon!"

"Leave dragon slaying to men who know how to fight, boy. Go home to your father."

"The girl put on a better show than he did!"

George did his best to ignore the ribbing, but the last comment hit home. In his battle lust, he'd forgotten about his fairy godmother, Lady Zoraida, who'd graciously agreed to be the maiden bait who tempted the dragon out of its cave. If she'd been injured by the dragon, he'd never forgive himself.

"Where's the girl? What happened to her?" George blurted out, finally allowing himself to peer back down the hill to where the dragon's cave lay.

"Held up her end of the fight better'n you, boy. Threw some of the dragon's own fire back at him, she did. He didn't like that, neither. He tried to eat her, but she drew a big purple circle in the air and disappeared. Don't know why. She was holding her own against the dread beast, and no mistake. Maybe she didn't want to be a hero. I mean, who ever heard of a maiden who defeated a dragon?"

George opened his mouth to say that his saintly namesake had needed the help of a maiden to defeat his dragon, but he closed it again. The city guardsmen didn't want to hear stories about how other dragons had died — they wanted to witness the death of this one, which had terrorised their town for too long.

Instead, George said, "If you do, I want to meet her."

He'd apologise to Lady Zoraida when he saw her next, George promised himself, though it would probably be a while before he did. She hadn't been happy about helping him with the dragon, and he'd lost the enchanted sword she'd given him, too.

He had no luck with women or dragons.

Sighing deeply, George trudged home.

Seeing as he was still alive and there were a few hours of daylight left, he should help his father in the shop. More monster slaying could wait until the morrow.

Two

Melitta would never forget the day she decided she would become a hero. It was the holy day of St John, and the entire court was present in the Great Hall for the feast.

"Your Majesties, may I present to you, the renowned knight from far off lands, the hero of countless battles, the mighty Sir Chase!" the herald bellowed.

From her place at the high table, two seats away from Queen Margareta, Melitta had an ideal view of the knight who strode into the

Great Hall, haloed by the rosy rays of the sinking sun behind him. His armour caught the candlelight from all directions, bathing him in gold. Gasps rose from the long tables on either side of him. Only the king and his knights could afford so much metal, while most of them wore leather. To wear such glorious armour, for surely it could not be real gold, this travelling knight must be rich indeed. And if it was real gold…why, he must be the best knight in all the lands, and a true hero.

The kind she wished to be.

King Erik called for a place to be set for the knight, before announcing grandly that there should be a tourney on the morrow, so that his own men could test their skill against such a legendary hero.

Cheers erupted around the hall and men raised their cups to toast the king's health.

Melitta didn't need to read the men's minds to know they all shared the same thought: every man present wanted to beat the newcomer in a fair fight, for honour won in battle, even a mock battle, was more precious than life itself.

"Fools," Queen Margareta muttered to Mother, loud enough for Melitta to hear. Whether she included her husband in that, Melitta didn't know.

As if the knight had heard, Sir Chase bowed his head and removed his helmet.

Now it was Melitta's turn to gasp.

Sir Chase was the handsomest man she had ever seen. Dark hair warred with light coloured eyes, and yet the outcome of the battle was…mesmerising. No wrinkle or a scar marked his face, beneath a thatch that bore not even a single white hair. He appeared younger than even their ever-youthful queen. Too young to be a hero, yet here he was.

Sir Chase bowed low before the dais. "Your Majesty King Erik, I am honoured by your hospitality. I wish only to serve."

This was when he would whip out his sword and lay it at the king's feet, Melitta knew, as he pledged his fealty and honour to the king's service. She'd seen enough knights sworn in to know the way of it.

Yet Sir Chase's sword remained firmly in its scabbard.

"I eagerly await tomorrow's tourney, for what better way to show a man's fighting prowess? Yet there is more to a knight than his sword."

Queen Margareta's musical laughter rang out across the hall, silencing all conversation. "Pray continue, Sir Knight."

"As you wish, most beautiful queen. A true hero must keep his wits as sharp as his blade. His honour must shine as bright as his armour, and never be allowed to tarnish. So that if his liege or his lady is plagued by the most enormous monster or the tiniest gnat, he can dispatch it forthwith."

Gnats? In summertime, they had more problems with flies, Melitta thought, shooing several of the buzzing nuisances away from her meat. How did they manage to seek her out so fast? She'd been so focussed on Sir Chase she hadn't seen them appear.

"Allow me, Your Majesty," Sir Chase said.

He reached behind him for his bow, notched an arrow to the string and let it fly. His arrow lodged in one of the tapestries high above Melitta's head.

What was he doing? In her momentary distraction, Melitta must have missed something Sir Chase had said.

Melitta bit her lip, and concentrated on his thoughts.

His gaze centred on a fly buzzing above the queen's head as he drew another arrow. The point followed the insect until he had a clear shot, when the knight released. His arrow arced up, skewering the insect before embedding itself in the wax encrusting a lit candelabra at the back of the dais. The candles wobbled for a moment, but did not fall, to the knight's relief.

Evidently deciding that Melitta's meal was a far safer target than the queen's, a fly zoomed past Melitta's face.

For a single, heart-stopping moment, Sir Chase's eyes met Melitta's. His eyelid drooped in what was definitely a wink.

She clearly heard him say, "Fear not, young maiden. A knight's duty is to save every lady, not just the queen."

His arrow point followed the fly as it finally left her alone and bumbled toward Mother.

Melitta felt a burst of satisfaction from the knight as he released the third arrow. It would meet its target, the queen would be impressed, he would have a place at court, he…

Queen Margareta leaped to her feet. "Guards!"

Melitta stared. A thin line of blood trickled down the queen's fingers to where the arrow had lodged in the table before her. A shimmery wing was all that remained of the fly, now squashed under the weight of the arrow point. The knight had shot the bug, all right, but he'd been so intent on his target that he'd unwittingly hurt the queen.

Sir Chase was too stunned to resist as two

of the king's trusted men seized his arms, and a third reached for his sword. "Your Majesty, I meant…I meant to rid you of a pest, not…" Sir Chase stammered.

"Silence!" Queen Margareta thundered.

At her side, King Erik rose. "Anyone who seeks to harm my queen commits treason. Such a heinous crime is punishable by death."

Sir Chase's thoughts were a jumbled mess of panic as he found he could not speak. Yet rising through it all was a scream of horror that he had not meant to harm the queen. Melitta believed him.

But the queen did not.

"He's telling the truth!" Melitta was surprised to hear her own high voice echo across the hall. Somehow, she'd risen from her seat, and now her knees wanted to wilt so that she could sink under the table and hide from what seemed like every eye turned toward her. Yet Sir Chase's talk of honour and heroes emboldened her, and she forced herself to stand tall. Maidens could be heroes, too. "He shot a fly. Look!" She pointed at the arrow with a hand that shook.

Mother shoved her back into her seat, telling her to hush, but it was too late. The queen had heard every word.

Glittering dark eyes seemed to survey Melitta's soul. Melitta stared back defiantly. Until, miracle of miracles, the queen inclined her head and yielded.

Queen Margareta turned to the knight. "Get out," she said softly. "This once, you may leave with your life. Set foot in this kingdom again and you will not be so lucky."

Melitta slid out of the knight's mind as easily as she'd ventured into it. He bowed one last time toward the dais before making a hasty exit. And while Sir Chase vanished from her world, he never really left her thoughts.

Only it wasn't his handsome face, or his shiny armour that stayed with her. No, it was his words. And the dead flies.

And the hope, one day, of being a hero once more.

Three

George's father looked up from the boot he was piecing together. "Dragon watching again, hmm?"

Not wanting to talk about his horrible failure any more, George simply nodded. He considered helping his father with the boot's fellow, but he was too weary for the kind of precision it required. Instead, he spread a piece of leather out on the cutting table. Destruction was more his style today. George reached for a pair of shears and set to work cutting out soles for shoes.

"Who was today's challenger?" Father asked.

It was too much to ask that Father had been too busy working to hear the dragon roaring.

George snipped savagely. "No one of consequence."

Father nodded sagely as the boot took a distinct curve in his hands. George would always envy the nimbleness of his father's fingers, forming such beautifully shaped shoes from a flat piece of leather. "So your dragon is alive and well, then? How about the would-be slayer?"

"Alive," George bit out as he snipped the sole free. "He ran away." Because he was outmatched, George snarled inwardly. Better to run away and fight properly another day.

"A smart slayer. Will wonders never cease?" Father lifted a needle to his eye and threaded it in one smooth stroke. "That's who will rid us of that nuisance. Not some mighty hero with a stout sword and shiny armour, but a man with a powerful mind. Dragons are cunning creatures, and fighting one will always be a battle of wits."

"I wish more people listened to your good advice, Father," George said, wishing he had. When his father found out his own son had been today's idiot, George intended to make himself scarce. "I don't think I'll watch the next challenger fight the dragon. I'll stay here and help you instead. There's a lot of orders here. Will we get them done in time?"

Father held up a finished upper, ready to stitch to the sole George had cut. "Together, I'm sure we will. Your mother would be proud."

George winced. If his mother was still alive, his father wouldn't need him in the shop so much. And she would have forbidden him from going anywhere near the dragon, let alone attempting to fight it. Even his fairy godmother had tried to talk him out of it, but he'd been too stupid to listen.

George snipped around another sole. Zoraida had been better at battling the dragon than he had, and his mother had had more wits than any man alive, or so his father said. Perhaps that was how his namesake had defeated that long-ago dragon. The stories all said he'd saved the virgin princess from the beast, but maybe she'd defeated the dragon and all he'd done was offer her his cloak to cover her singed clothes. The townspeople had proclaimed him a hero and not believed a girl could beat the beast.

For who had ever heard of a maiden hero? Not George. He'd like to meet one, though. Such a paragon might be able to tell him what he was doing wrong.

He sighed and set down his shears. No, she probably wouldn't even notice some lowly shoemaker's son. She'd be inundated by marriage proposals from every prince, knight and nobleman for miles around. For a woman who could best a dragon would also bear brave sons.

Or so they said.

If only he'd inherited his mother's wits.

Then he'd know how to best a dragon in battle…

Four

After St John's Day, Melitta resolved to spend more time on archery. She dusted off her bow, took a few minutes to remember how to string it, then headed to the field reserved for the archery butts. It appeared that everyone else shared her passion for archery practice, for the normally deserted butts now had queues of men and boys waiting their turn.

Everyone in the training grounds seemed to want to best Sir Chase at his fly-shooting, even if the knight himself had departed in accordance with the queen's command. While they were waiting, a bunch of boys Melitta's age had climbed the fence into the next field and were shooting at a pile of horse dung.

"I got that one!" one boy cried excitedly.

"No, you didn't," another boy snapped, looking like a smaller version of the boy he'd contradicted. Brothers, Melitta assumed. "It just flew away and you didn't see it."

"Watch where you're shooting!" cried a third boy, as horse dung splattered his shoes.

"You're aiming too low," Melitta said, jerking her chin at the boy who'd caused the splatter. "When they notice movement, they fly up and off. So you need to aim higher, for where they're going to be."

The boy she'd tried to help glared at her. "What would a girl know about archery?"

His friends joined in.

"Yeah, what would a girl know?"

"Girls can't be knights!"

"Girls don't belong in the practice yard."

"Shouldn't you be in some chamber

somewhere, practising your sewing?"

Melitta regarded the boys coolly. "I'm already better at sewing than you are at archery. Maybe you all would be better off inside sewing."

"What's going on here?" The deeper voice of a man cut through the boys' enraged protests. The master-at-arms, Sir Faris. "Shouldn't you boys be practising, instead of flirting with girls?"

More shouting ensued, until Sir Faris waved the boys into silence.

"What are you doing here?" the knight asked Melitta.

She lifted her bow. "Waiting for my turn to practice."

Sir Faris' eyebrows rose. "Is King Erik's army so weak we need girls to man the walls? I see more fighting men here than any other kingdom in the world can boast. We would be in dire straits indeed if we had to rely on girls to protect the castle."

"Queen Margareta once protected the king

from a dozen men," Melitta returned. She had heard the tale many times.

"Is that the tale your mother tells you? I heard the queen distracted the men with her womanly charms so that the king could slay them and lay their bodies at her feet for daring to attack her." Sir Faris' gaze held pity. "Girls on the practice field or the battlefield are little more than a distraction. Go home to your mother, child."

Melitta met his gaze. "My mother is with the queen, and she shall hear of this. After I have had my turn at the butts. I have as much right as any man here."

Any pity Sir Faris had shown vanished. "Then pick a queue, girl, and be prepared to wait a while. My men have been here since dawn, when a little lady like yourself was fast asleep in her bed." He stalked away, cupping his hands to his mouth to shout instructions to a man sighting on the furthest target.

Melitta surveyed the field. At this rate, it would be several hours before the men tired of archery and let her anywhere near the butts. In the meantime, she could stand around, watching, or she could join the boys in shooting shit. Neither appealed to her. Sure, she could carry out her threat and tell the queen what had transpired, but she knew her mother was working on a dress for the young princess's betrothal ceremony, and if Melitta joined them, she'd soon find her hands full of pins and silk. So much for her hopes of being a hero.

Melitta marched to the armoury, resolving to put her bow away until later in the evening, when the men were gone. She wasn't giving up, she told herself. Merely postponing practice.

The armour-master was nowhere to be seen, but Melitta heard a clatter from the darkness at the back of the cavernous cellar that housed King Erik's armoury. "Sir Bruno?" Melitta ventured.

"What is it, boy?" a gruff voice demanded. Sir Bruno, the armour-master, emerged from the darkness carrying a pile of shields almost as high as his head. "Who are you?"

"Lady Melitta, Lady Penelope's daughter," Melitta replied. From girl to child to boy, Melitta had had enough of diminutives for one day.

Sir Bruno scratched his bald pate. "What can I do for you, my lady?" Before she could respond, the stack of shields unbalanced and clattered to the floor. Sir Bruno growled out a string of colourful curses, only half of which Melitta understood.

One of the shields rolled, hit the wall and toppled over at her feet. Melitta reached down to pick it up and was struck with the design on the round shield. Concentric circles, much like the archery targets outside. A dark stain marred the design. "What are you doing with these?" she asked.

"Throwing them out, milady. Some of these are centuries old, captured from Viking raiders, and no use to anyone. Even if they weren't mouldy like the one you hold, lady." Sir Bruno reached for the offending item.

Melitta clutched it to her chest. "So if I wanted to use it for an archery target, no one would mind?"

Sir Bruno laughed. "If you were to throw it in the fire, not even the king himself would object, my lady."

"Good." Melitta surveyed the mess. "May I have another?"

"You may have them all. As many as you can carry." Sir Bruno laughed.

Oh, so he thought a girl couldn't lift a shield or two? Melitta fumed. Bolts of silk might not seem like much until you had to carry them halfway across the castle to the queen's chambers, up and down stairs until your arms ached. She selected two more and hefted all three in her arms. Heavy, yes, but no heavier than an armload of silks for her mother. "Thank you," she said sweetly, hitching her quiver higher on her shoulder as she turned to go.

"Any time, my lady," Sir Bruno called after

her.

Five

Melitta set up her practice range in the corridor outside her mother's apartments. She wedged her shield target in the window, then stood back to take aim. Her first arrow hit the wall and clattered to the stone floor with a sound reminiscent of mocking applause.

Practice, Melitta told herself. The more practice she got, the better she'd become.

By the end of the morning, she could at least hit the target on every shot. She hadn't forgotten how to shoot, at least. She kept at it until she managed to hit the white circle in the centre three times in a row. Only then did she set down her bow to massage her aching fingers. It wasn't enough. She'd have to soak them.

Melitta headed inside her chamber, intent on finding a jug of water. She immersed her whole hand in the one on the table, beside the dinner a maid had delivered for her hours ago. Only now did she realise how hungry she was.

As she devoured her dinner, Melitta mused that there must be a simpler way to heroism than hours of archery practice. Her fingers would be a mess of callouses before the week was out – she wouldn't be able to sew a stitch. Her mother would not be happy.

Too bad. Lady Penelope had made her own choices in life. Melitta was old enough to marry, which meant she got to make choices, too. If she chose not to spend her whole life at a loom like her mother, it was her choice.

Melitta tore off a piece of bread and dipped it into the dish of honey. The movement set off a small swarm of flies that she hadn't seen until now.

Dropping her bread in disgust, Melitta reached for her quiver. At this distance, she could stab the flies with the point of her arrow – no bow required. Yet her fingers closed on the strap that held the quiver to her shoulder. There was a faster way to swat flies that didn't require a bow or arrow.

Carefully, she raised the strap. The flies buzzed on, oblivious. One or two even settled on the surface of the honey once more.

Melitta took a deep breath, then struck. The strap slapped against the table, making her tray jump before it landed with a clatter. For all the noise, it didn't look like she'd caught a single one. Chagrined, Melitta flipped over the strap to see if she'd perhaps caught a particularly slow fly.

She counted. Then counted again. No, surely not. After a third count, the strap dropped from her nerveless fingers. "A dozen," she breathed in disbelief. "A dozen dead with a single blow. Take that, Sir Faris and anyone else who says a girl has no place in battle. Sir Chase killed them one at a time, yet I can take a dozen in a single stroke!"

Seizing the strip of leather, she took the steps two at a time to the practice range. Most of the men had gone, but the boys were still there, taking their turn on the butts.

"You're wasting your time!" she called, flapping the strap. "You're using the wrong weapon! Look, I killed a dozen in a single blow!"

"Let me see that, girl." Sir Faris seized the strap. "A dozen currants? Deadly foes, indeed!" He laughed, and the boys joined in.

"They are not currants, or any kind of fruit," Melitta snapped. "They're flies, the same as the ones they've been trying to shoot all morning. I killed a dozen with one blow. More than even the great knight yesterday managed to do!"

"The one the queen threw out of the kingdom? He wasn't so great," one of the boys mocked to more laughter.

Melitta folded her arms across her chest. "So you say, yet all of you are out here, working on your bow skills so you can do better than him. Well, you've been bested by a girl. How many of you can kill a dozen with one blow?"

The boys howled with laughter.

Sir Faris laid a hand on her shoulder. "They have the right of it, girl. Catching flies will never win a battle, and a knight who thinks so is little more than entertainment at a feast. Forget your dozen and do something more suited to your station."

Melitta shrugged off his hand and stalked away. Sir Faris was wrong, she swore to herself, and one day she would prove it to him, and the world.

Six

"Are you sure you aren't coming? This could make our fortunes, you know," Father said, hefting another chest into the already full cart.

And make shoes for the rest of his life? George shook his head. "I'm sure, Father. I want a chance at adventure. If I fail…well, I will know where to find you, to ask for a job."

Father patted the horse as he passed. "Of course you will. This Shoetown is where the forest meets the desert, far to the south. In a land where the court ladies dance through a pair of slippers each and every night. A land where a shoemaker might fancy himself a king."

George laughed. "Where you will make yourself as rich as a king, you mean. The rest of it – the business of ruling a kingdom and keeping the neighbouring kingdoms from invading – is more trouble than it's worth, I'm sure."

Father rested his hands on George's shoulders. It rankled that George wasn't as tall as his father yet, and might never be. "Some might say the same of an adventurer's life. Slaying monsters is more trouble than it's worth, as you've already learned."

George's heart sank. His father had been strangely silent about his battle with the dragon, though he had to have heard about his crushing failure. The whole city and surrounding countryside knew. Still, George summoned a smile. "What is it you and Mother used to tell me when I was small and learning to make shoes in the workshop? Your first attempt will fail. Yet I had to keep trying until I succeeded. No matter how many times I failed. Because it's about learning to do it right, so you don't fail any more."

Father's smile looked just as forced. "Just as long as you live long enough to keep trying until you succeed. Shoes are not as dangerous as dragons."

"I know." George met his father's gaze without flinching. His resolve didn't waver, despite the ache in his heart at having to farewell his father.

Father climbed onto the cart. "When you have slayed the beast, come and find me. I promise to make you boots from the beast's hide."

If the dragon didn't make a meal of his own hide instead. A lump formed in George's throat. His father had more confidence in him than George had for himself. "You can count on it," George said.

They exchanged a long look, where not a word was said. Least of all the fateful farewell.

It only ended when Father tapped the horse with his whip, urging it forward. The moment shattered, and they parted ways, perhaps for the last time.

Seven

Despite Melitta's best efforts, tales of her fly-killing achievements reached every corner of the castle within a day. She could not set foot outside her mother's apartments without someone mentioning a dozen with one blow, before they dissolved into laughter. So she shut herself in with her sewing.

"Ooh, is that a new gown for the queen?" an excited voice asked.

Melitta glanced up to find Inga, one of the maids, staring avidly at her. Given she was working on blue silk, which only the queen wore, on any normal occasion, the question would have been quite a silly one. However, under the circumstances…

"No," Melitta replied. "This is the princess's betrothal gown. The king wants her to wear white, but the queen insists the gown be blue. Mother had some blue silk so pale it almost looks white, which met with Queen Margareta's approval, so I get to make it while Mother makes the queen's gown."

Inga nodded. "Lady Penelope makes the most beautiful gowns."

Melitta couldn't disagree. Her mother could take cloth and thread and turn it into something magical. Moreover, Mother seemed to actually enjoy creating clothing.

She'd once travelled the world with her husband, Sir Godfrey, until Melitta's father had nobly sacrificed his life to save a convent from a bunch of barbarians, or so Mother said when she told the tale. He'd earned himself sainthood as a result, for thanks to his sacrifice, none of the novices were harmed by the barbarians, when a miracle turned them into birds and they flew away.

It was such a far-fetched tale, Melitta wouldn't have believed it, if the nuns in the convent where she'd spent her earliest years hadn't sworn to its veracity. Some had even been witnesses to the events of that day, and Melitta had seen it in their thoughts. Not that she was the sort of witch who could turn men into birds – oh, no. Mind reading was the questionable gift she had inherited from her mother, though she rarely used it.

Without Melitta having to tell her, Queen Margareta heard the tale of Sir Faris' remarks on the training ground, and her response was everything Melitta could have hoped for.

Though the queen never so much as touched a sword, it was well known that she was as deadly as the king. She had summoned Sir Faris to the throne room to answer why he had not allowed a girl to enter the practice fields. She'd insisted that in ancient times, women had trained just as rigorously as men, for women were as likely to die at the point of a blade as any man, so they had a right to learn to use any weapon they could handle. When he began to protest that having women present would distract the men, an excuse quickly picked up and seconded by some of the other noblemen present, she'd shaken her head that her king's troops were so weak. Why, all an enemy army had to do was bring a woman with them and they would be undone, which simply would not do.

Then she'd sweetly offered to stand on the training ground herself until men learned not to be distracted. And she'd do it naked.

Silence had descended on the court for a long moment. Melitta didn't need to read the men's minds to see the lust burning in their eyes. The queen's beauty was enough to halt an army in its tracks, even without taking into account her magical powers.

At that point, King Erik had waded into the fray in her support. Most said it was to protect the queen's modesty, or some such noble thought, but Mother had muttered that it was more about keeping his men alive. Men lost their minds over the queen in ways they never would for Melitta.

So Melitta spent her mornings in the practice yard, ignoring the laughter as she learned how to hold a sword without dropping it. By the end of a week, she considered herself a passable swordswoman who could manage an occasional bout against one of the young squires without falling on her backside. She'd even won a few, amid grumbling from the boys.

Sure, she might not be a hero yet, but she intended to do everything in her power to be ready when the opportunity came. She would not spend a lifetime sewing clothes for a court who didn't care a jot about her. At least, not until she'd had her fair share of adventure, like her mother had.

Eight

When George set out from his father's house, he had a fool-proof plan, or so he thought. Unless he was a fool for thinking it up, which was always possible.

Somewhere, there were other would-be heroes. Others who wished to slay dragons. He would journey to another town where no one had heard of his defeat, and make it known that he wished to engage an apprentice. An apprentice hero, if there were such a thing. Perhaps even several, if he could find enough suitable boys. He didn't dare hope for a girl like his fairy godmother, and yet…he'd seen dozens of men challenge the dragon, but he alone among them had survived by running away. And he'd managed that only because Zoraida battled the dragon alone, distracting the beast.

He'd take up residence in the best inn in town, and pay the town crier to shout his news to all who would hear it for a few days. Then, he'd have applicants lining up across the town square, he was certain of it.

He'd even made up some signs he would nail to the outside of the inn, for those who could read. After all, if his father was right and a man needed more brain than brawn to beat a dragon, then an educated apprentice would be a wise choice.

He unrolled the signs on the table, surveying the top one with a critical eye. He hoped it would be enticing enough. He'd drawn the dragon himself, and his drawing skills had never been the best.

Heroes wanted, the poster read, for monster slaying of all kinds. Apply within.

"Are you looking for a hero, boy?"

George looked up. The man who met his gaze looked like one of the knights who'd died trying to defeat the dragon. A hero, in other words.

A hero who would claim all the glory, if they were to team up to kill the beast, George's traitorous mind added.

"Where's the dragon and what's the reward?" the man asked, turning the poster so the writing was right way up.

"Kasmirus, between the city and the river," George admitted. "But I don't know the reward. Every time it kills another knight, the king increases it."

"How big is the beast, and does it breathe fire?"

George swallowed. "It would scarcely fit in the square outside, and its fiery breath is so hot, it has been known to melt a man's armour."

The man considered the scroll for a long moment, then rolled it up. "Which means it's impossible to kill."

"Not impossible," George countered. "All creatures must die some time."

The man grinned. "Even us. But there's nothing heroic about being roasted alive. I'm Sir Chase." He held out his hand.

"George," he said, clasping the knight's arm briefly before letting go.

Sir Chase gestured to the innkeeper. "Two more ales for me and my friend here!" When the innkeeper nodded, Chase turned back to George. "Where are you headed?"

"Aros," George said. It was the nearest large town to Kasmirus, though hopefully far enough for no one to have heard of him before.

Sir Chase started, his eyes widening in horror for a moment before his expression relaxed into a smile again. "Not a good city for heroes, Aros. Their queen isn't fond of adventurers."

George raised his eyebrows. "That's not what I heard. When they hold tourneys, the queen richly rewards the victor. She holds heroes in high regard, or so it is said." And a kingdom where its queen held so much power was the most likely place to find a girl who would answer his call for a hero, George thought but did not say.

Sir Chase choked on his ale. Wiping his mouth with the back of his hand, he said, "Aye, I heard the same. Until I met the woman. Beautiful as the day is long, but cold as ice. Looking into her eyes is enough to freeze your soul, and no mistake."

George paused for a moment, considering. Was he wrong to head for Aros? Perhaps he should travel further to another city.

No, he decided. What was a queen to him? He wanted to recruit some of her subjects, not meet the woman or even set foot in her court. "Then I'll be sure to avoid her," George said finally.

"Wise choice." Sir Chase raised his ale. "And

I will avoid your dragon. I heard about a pack of troublesome wolves in the north. I might go see to those instead."

George clunked his cup against the knight's. "To both our good health, and long lives," he said gravely, and drank.

As he drained his drink, George prayed that he wasn't making the wrong decision in heading for Aros. Only time would tell.

Nine

Every squire in the bailey was talking or thinking about the apprenticeship, Melitta was certain of it. She'd even ventured to read some thoughts to confirm it. The hero would have a hundred applicants before the week was out, and every single one of them bigger, stronger and better with a sword than she was, or would ever be. The only thing she was better at was…sewing, not a talent in high regard among heroes.

Unless she could sew herself a heroic

reputation in the next few days, Melitta didn't stand a chance.

On the morrow, the line stretched from the tavern to the city gates, as every likely lad vied for the chance to be a hero's apprentice. Some wore little more than rags, but for once, they shared something with the simply dressed tradesmen's sons and the noble boys in their leather armour, mail and emblazoned silk surcoats: their eyes were filled with hope.

Any hope Melitta had harboured died at the sight. She hadn't any chance of being chosen. It wasn't like she even knew what their family emblem was to embroider it on a surcoat.

"What is our family crest?" Melitta asked her mother.

Mother's loom continued its steady pace. "We have none. My family came from a court where we had no need of such things — a name was enough. And your father…to tell you the truth, I cannot remember. He wore the sign of a cross for the holy crusade he was on, so I never saw any other symbol on him."

"But we should have one. Maybe it wasn't the done thing where you came from, but everyone else at court has their heraldry," Melitta pressed.

Mother laughed. "Why? Are you thinking of fighting in a tourney and wearing your own colours? Tell me you're not as silly as all those boys lined up outside."

"Being a hero is not silly. Some people would say making pretty clothes is silly," Melitta retorted. The moment the words left her lips, she regretted them, but it was too late.

Mother's loom clicked into ominous silence. "We are ladies of the court. We set the tone for fashion and dress amongst the highest in the land. The courts of other kingdoms look to us for what to wear. For new ways to fashion fur and fabric. If you find all your silk dresses so silly, perhaps you should wear a sack instead."

Now Melitta felt even worse. "I didn't mean
– "

"Or is it armour you want? After killing a

dozen with one blow, you feel your hands are better employed with something sharper than a needle? Do you want to join those boys out there, wishing for something that will only get them killed like your father was?" A tear stood bright on Mother's cheek.

"I'm sorry, Mother," Melitta said quietly. "I'm not as reckless as that. I just wish for more to life than clothes and maybe marriage."

Mother wiped her tears away. "I know you aren't your father, but you're all I have left. And sometimes you remind me of him so much…when you don't remind me of me." She sniffed with what Melitta thought sounded like finality. "When I was a girl, I wanted to be an assassin, like one of the Sultan's daughters. Then my mother gave me this awful gown that I couldn't stand, so I unstitched it, dyed it anew and remade that gown until I could bear to wear it. My own mother didn't recognise it. And then I met your father…and found a new passion." She sighed. "I know you don't share my passion for creating cloth and clothing. I had hoped you might find something else you enjoyed. Heaven knows you've sneaked into enough places in the palace to have tried everything that you could."

"But not slaying monsters," Melitta said.

Mother laughed weakly. "I'm not sure there are any monsters left in the world to slay. All the monsters I've met have been human, and you aren't an assassin any more than I am. Could you kill a man, Melitta?"

Melitta herself didn't know the answer to that. "If I had to, I suppose," she said. Remembering the flies, she perked up. "I did kill a dozen with one blow. That knight who came to the feast would say it shows the mark of a true warrior."

"Then I shall make you a surcoat with new colours, that says what a hero you already are. And on the morrow you can walk past those hordes of boys, putting them to shame," Mother said.

Now Melitta's eyes threatened tears. "Even after what happened to Father, you would let me apprentice myself to a hero as a slayer of monsters?"

Mother's smile seemed forced, but her words rang true. "If your passion is for monsters, I cannot stop you from pursuing it. My parents never wanted me to marry your father, but I gave them no choice in the matter." She rose and headed for the chest where she kept her best silks. "So, what colours would you like to wear, my young warrior?"

Melitta thought for a moment. "What do we have that is closest to honey?"

Ten

When he saw the queue outside the tavern in the morning, George thanked his lucky stars. He would have an apprentice to help him in no time – that dragon was as good as dead. Aros had been the right place to go, after all.

Yet as each boy walked into the private room he'd rented in the tavern, he began to have doubts.

"Wrong room."

"You're no hero!"

"Why, you're younger than me, and smaller

to boot!"

It seemed tales of his failure at home had indeed spread to this city, too. At this rate, he'd have to try another town even further away to find someone who hadn't heard of his disastrous dragon battle.

As the light through the window turned rosy, George prepared to pack up and move on. The line that had held such hopes for him this morning was non-existent. The last boy had crushed his hopes under his hobnailed boots.

"Excuse me?"

George looked up at the distinctly feminine voice.

"I heard there was a place for an apprentice hero?" The girl — or perhaps a particularly skinny boy, George thought, though he doubted it — sidled into the room. She'd cut her hair like a pageboy, but she looked old enough to be a squire. Clad in a tunic and hose that were too well-made to belong to a peasant, she wore them like they were her own, and not borrowed from one of her brothers. Practical clothing, suitable for fighting in a practice yard. The only bit of finery she wore was a flame-coloured surcoat, embroidered with words George couldn't quite make out.

Then she turned, and it came clear. "A dozen at one blow," he read. He eyed the girl, whose slender arms couldn't have wielded anything larger than a dagger in her life. "I don't believe it."

She set her hands on her hips. "Ask anyone in town. One blow and I had a dozen dead. Just like that." For a moment, it seemed like fire burned in her eyes.

George was mesmerised. She reminded him of his fairy godmother. Only closer to his age.

He shook himself. This girl couldn't help him defeat the dragon. He needed a better warrior than he was.

"Innkeep!" George shouted.

The innkeeper stuck his head in the room. "More ale?"

"Yes," he said. "But first…have you ever heard of anyone who can kill a dozen with a single blow?"

The innkeeper grinned broadly. "You mean Melitta here? How can a hero as big as you not hear of such things? You'd better not show any disrespect, or you'll be number thirteen!" He left, laughing.

The girl looked incensed. "Do you believe me now?"

She didn't look like a killer, but then, Zoraida hadn't looked like a fairy godmother, either. Especially not while battling a dragon. And Zoraida had held her own against the beast.

"Are you afraid of dragons?" George demanded.

"I'm not afraid of anything," she insisted.

"Have you ever met a dragon?" he pressed.

Doubt flickered over her features.

The answer to his question was no.

"Have you ever run away from a fight?" George asked.

She snorted. "Of course not."

Unmanned by a girl. George dismissed the thought as quickly as it had come.

"Can you handle a sword?" he asked.

"Tolerably in the practice yard," she said. "I'm better with a bow and I can ride."

George was in love. Standing before him was the perfect woman.

"And I think you should choose me for your apprentice," she finished. She eyed him. "But I'm not going to sleep with you."

Apprentice? All George's dreams of getting her into bed sputtered and died. Had she read his thoughts?

"Yes," she replied. "A minor inconvenience I inherited from my mother. That and a fairy godmother."

The wheels in George's mind started turning. The two of them, plus two fairy godmothers. Between the four of them, they might be able to best that dragon.

"You're hired," he said.

Eleven

Melitta's feet felt like they were floating all the way back to her mother's apartments. Out of all the would-be heroes, boys who were far better with a bow and a sword, he had picked her! She couldn't wait to start her training. Wondering what kind of monster Sir George would test her with first, Melitta dreamed of dragons as she packed her things. Her dresses would stay, of course – silk skirts would only get in the way in a fight.

Melitta thought to fill a chest with her

things, but by the time she had assembled all of her suitable fighting clothes, they took up scarcely a quarter of the space in the smallest chest her mother owned. She would be better served with a sack, or a saddlebag. Perhaps…

"So, the rumours are true? The whole castle is buzzing with the news that the hero chose a girl as his apprentice. And not just any girl…you." Mother loomed in the doorway, her hands on her hips as though she planned to block her daughter's exit.

Melitta couldn't keep the pride out of her voice. "Yes, he did," she said. "And he believes I can kill a dragon. I saw it in his thoughts."

Mother's frightening figure seemed to shrink as she sank onto a chair. "I don't believe it," she said weakly. "All those boys, squires, knights in training…and he chose you?"

"Yes, Mother." Melitta wondered where she might find a suitable sack. Perhaps in the kitchens.

"He must think you are a doxy, a whore who will leap into his bed the moment he commands it," Mother declared. "You must send word to his lodgings that you are no such thing, and as a lady of the court, you will have no further dealings with such a dishonourable man."

Melitta grinned. "He did think about me naked for a moment, but when I told him I would never sleep with him, he seemed resigned to it. He truly offered me the apprenticeship because he believes I have the makings of a hero."

Mother let out a sigh, deflating in defeat. "But are you sure this is what you want? I had plenty of adventures in my youth, particularly after I met your father. But never once did I have to take up a sword, or fight a monster who was stronger than a man. Even then…" Mother swallowed. She continued, "I thought you wanted to meet this hero because, well…you are of marriageable age. I saw how you looked at the knight the queen banished, and it made me realise… I was about your age when I met your father. Your age when I chose my husband. It is plain that no man at court has caught your eye, but a newcomer with an eye for adventure…Why, were I younger, I would find him difficult to resist." She laughed, blushing.

Marriage? Melitta recoiled at the very idea. "No," she said decidedly. "I am not in love with Sir George. Or Sir Chase, though I admit he was a handsome fellow."

"I could speak to the queen," Mother began eagerly. "Perhaps you will know of a suitable man. Not someone at court, but perhaps one of King Eric's bannermen…"

Melitta curled her lip. "And have her marry me off to some chubby cheeked prince where I will be forced to pop out babies, in between weaving and sewing until my womb and hands no longer work? No, thank you. I wish to live a little before I am chained to a birthing bed."

"Perhaps a widower who already has children. Enough heirs that you need not breed at all," Mother suggested, but Melitta didn't need to read her mind to know that her own mother didn't even believe she could do such a thing.

"I am not ready for marriage." Even as the words left her lips Melitta knew they were true. She wasn't. She might never be.

Mother bowed her head. "I know," she admitted. She took a deep breath. "Which is why, though it breaks my heart to do it, I shall allow you to go with my blessing. And a warning. Whatever monsters you choose to kill, never attempt to cross a mermaid."

Melitta managed a smile. As a mind reader, she knew the queen's secret as well as her mother did. "For Queen Margareta will never forgive me."

Little more of consequence passed between her and her mother until her departure on the morrow. Melitta and her mother packed her things, and it seemed like no time at all before Melitta mounted her gelding and said farewell.

Farewell to the life she had lived, as she rode through the gates on the first step of her journey to become a legendary hero.

Or so she hoped.

Twelve

After a week of travelling, staying in a different inn every night, Melitta finally worked up the courage to ask George, "So where is this dragon we're going to kill?"

George took his time putting down his dagger and swallowing his mouthful of pork, before he answered, "We're not killing the dragon yet."

Melitta opened her mouth to ask why, but George cut her off.

"I've seen you practising on the targets in

the inn yards," he said. "You can handle a bow, though your marksmanship could do with some work. And you say you have killed a dozen, but I have not seen it. First, we should test your skills against something smaller. More manageable."

Melitta's heart sank. Killing flies was one thing, but something bigger, living, breathing… She swallowed. Melitta wasn't sure she could do it.

George pulled a crumpled piece of parchment from his saddlebag and unrolled it on the table. "There is a town two days' ride from here which has a wild boar problem. One beast in particular has a price on his head. So your first quest in training to be a hero will be to kill this pig and claim the reward." He sat back, lifting his tankard to his lips.

Melitta's blood ran cold. "A boar? A wild boar? A beast that looks like a pig on the outside, and may taste like one when it's dead and roasted, but while it lives, it is the receptacle of the devil's rage that few would stand against?"

"Are you afraid of a pig?"

Desperately, Melitta wanted to say no. But if she did, she knew it would be a lie. As one of the ladies of the court, she had often been allowed to accompany hunting parties. When the court hunted deer, fox, or the frequent hawking expeditions that the queen was so fond of. Melitta could watch the queen's falcon in flight all day, so graceful was the bird. But when King Erik had caught wind of a monstrous boar that he wished to hunt, Mother had forbidden it. Melitta had stood at the window, watching the hunting party leave without her, bitterness festering in her breast. There had been few ladies in that party, and all the men had carried spears instead of bows. It wasn't till much later, when the weary hunting party returned victorious, that Melitta realised why.

The beast had gored three knights - one fatally - before it had succumbed to the spear piercing its heart. By all accounts, the dead knight had saved King Erik's life, by leaping in front of the beast. When the queen had heard this, she forbade any future boar hunts. It might be King Erik's kingdom, but none disobeyed the queen.

Melitta swallowed. "We will need to be prepared," she said carefully. "We will need stout spears, for arrows will not be enough. I have never handled a spear, and I fear I may not have the strength to strike true before the beast is upon me."

George's eyes widened, as though she had surprised him. Good. "You've fought a boar before?"

"They are hunted by the king and his court," Melitta replied, pressing her lips together before he could make her spill the truth.

Sir George shook his head and appeared to regain his composure. "Then you have two days until we arrive in the town of Sanglier in which to formulate a plan for how you will kill the beast."

Two days? Two years would not be enough.

Melitta began to wish she had never left home in the first place.

Thirteen

During the two days' ride to Sanglier, Melitta scarcely uttered a word. Countless times, George had opened his mouth to comment on the weather, or ask her about herself, but he hadn't been able to make his tongue cooperate. He'd never met a girl who could incapacitate him so.

The one time he'd managed to hold a conversation with her, he'd told her about the Sanglier boar. He'd expected her to be afraid – Lord knew he was! – but she'd been as calm as still water as she described the best way to kill a boar.

With a spear. George didn't own a spear, and despite her admission that she had never fought with one, at least she'd seen one and knew what to do with it.

On reflection, he probably shouldn't have told her killing the beast would be up to her. Yet she'd sounded so knowledgeable, he'd been scared to tell her his plan, lest she scoff and call him a fool. He was the master and she was the apprentice, or at least that's the way it was supposed to be. There might be more to Melitta than he realised – and not just her fairy godmother, either.

Even if she was bluffing, which he doubted, if she got into trouble, she had but to call for her fairy godmother and she would have a powerful witch to save her. George knew his own fairy godmother was as likely to let him die as she was to save him, so he knew he couldn't count on any help from Zoraida. Not yet.

So as he sat down to the afternoon meal with Melitta, George ventured, "So what is your plan?"

Melitta glanced up at him, then directed her gaze at her bowl of stew. Haltingly at first, she began to tell him what had occupied her thoughts for the last two days.

George let out a low whistle. "That's not a bad plan at all. Let's see how it goes tonight."

Melitta paled. "Tonight?"

George didn't dare admit it to her, but staying at inns every night had taken all of his coin. If they didn't kill the boar tonight and claim its reward, he could not afford so much as a loaf of bread to break their fast in the morning.

He nodded gravely. "Tonight."

Fourteen

Looking down from her tree branch perch into the darkness below, Melitta repeated Sir George's words in her head. It wasn't a bad plan. It wasn't.

Then why did she feel like there were snakes writhing in her belly?

She shifted again, searching in vain for a comfortable spot on the hard tree branch. There was the trap, made of timber hastily nailed together this afternoon. It was barely visible in the moonlight now. The earthy smell of truffles and mushrooms filled the air, hopefully enough to entice the boar into the trap. If that bait wasn't enough, it sat at the foot of an oak tree, amid the remains of a century's worth of acorns.

Even Sir George had said the bait should be sufficient, but after several hours of sitting out here in the cold dark, Melitta wondered if perhaps they should have taken the advice of a man they met in the tavern. He had insisted that the only way to lure a pig was with the scent of fermented apples. Melitta had been on the verge of agreeing to include some apples in the bait, when the man had promptly offered to sell her a barrel of cider for a price higher than her mother would pay for a bale of silk. Yet now she was tempted to climb down from her tree, and venture to the tavern to see if she could acquire some of the overpriced cider. Anything to end her vigil.

Wait, was that movement?

Melitta squinted down the road. No, it was just the baker. He'd opened a window to set the rising bread dough on the windowsill. If he was baking already, then dawn would soon follow. The end of the night with no sign of their bloody boar, or sleep for her, either.

But wait…was that?

Yes!

A hulking shadow, low to the ground, passed in front of the bakery, ambling at a pace that showed the boar was in no hurry. Then it stopped and lifted its head so that its snout and tusks were clearly outlined against the light coming from the baker's window. Melitta's stomach lurched. Tusks like that could gut a man. She didn't even want to think of what it would do to her.

If he gored her, would the tusks go all the way through and come out her back?

She shut down that thought as quickly as it had come. Pigs couldn't climb trees, so she was safe up on her perch. She just had to wait for the animal to enter the trap, so that she could spring it, and the deed would be done.

She held her breath as the boar approached.

Still in no hurry, it paused to sniff the ground before taking a few steps and lowering its snout to the soil once more. Slowly, slowly fate was closing in on the beast. It was a good plan, just like Sir George had said.

Moonlight shimmered on the dew-dropped l eaves below her, before it abruptly winked out. The boar stood at the very entrance of their trap. Four steps would carry it all the way in, she decided, and then it would be trapped. No more terrorising the town for this pig.

Two steps. A long moment of snuffling, disturbing the moonlit leaves. Another step.

Melitta's lungs screamed for air, but she didn't dare inhale. Just one more, she begged the beast.

The beast trotted forward and buried its snout in a pile of mushrooms.

Melitta wanted to cheer, but she knew she couldn't. Not until the gate was closed. Now she tugged on the rope fastened to the gate below. It wasn't till she heard the latch click shut that she finally let herself breathe again. It was done. They'd captured the boar.

Sir George clambered down from his tree. Though he had said killing the boar was her task, in the end he had agreed to wield the spear that killed it.

So the knight took up a spear, hefting it in his hand as he approached the gate. The pig did not hear him at first, for it was too busy feasting on the bait. But he must've made some noise that alerted it, for the pig started, turned, and faced him.

Instead of throwing the spear directly into the pig's chest, as the beast presented him with the perfect target, George hesitated.

The pig did not. It charged at the gate. Which, to Melitta's horror, swung open. Somehow, it hadn't closed properly, and now the boar was no longer trapped, but it most certainly was enraged.

With a spear in his hand, George still stood in the perfect position to kill the beast. Melitta watched in awe, waiting.

George had other ideas. He took to his

heels and fled, with the boar not far behind.

Sir George was a coward? Melitta couldn't believe it, yet the evidence was right there before her eyes.

George headed for the only sanctuary either of them could see – the lit bakery. He wrenched open the door, and flung himself inside, but he didn't get a chance to shut the door before the boar followed him in.

A great commotion arose from the bakery, culminating in the door slamming shut. Which might have been good except both George and the boar was still inside.

Melitta crept down from her tree. She wasn't sure what to do, but she couldn't just sit there and do nothing. She snatched up the spare spears, and carried them to the bakery. She was George's assistant, after all, and if he needed more weapons, it was her job to provide them. And she might learn something from watching the battle, she told herself. She crept toward the lit window, the volume of the clatterings and crashes increasing with every step. Finally she was close enough to peer through the open shutters. She raised her head for scarcely a moment, before she had to duck to avoid being hit by the body flying out the window.

Sir George rolled, crouched, then clambered to his feet. He dusted himself off before he seized the spear from Melitta.

"That beast is going to die," he said through gritted teeth, advancing on the window.

But the boar, rampaging through the wrecked bakery, was hard to sight between the overturned tables and smashed furniture. Then it tore into a bag of flour and powder filled the air, making it even harder to see.

The beast shook its head, scattering flour everywhere, but it was unable to dislodge the bag from its tusks. It ran around madly, trampling everything in its path, until the bag finally flew off and landed in the fire. The empty flour sack began to smoke.

"There!" George hissed, loosing a spear. He caught the boar in the chest, but that didn't seem to slow the beast any. If anything, the pain only goaded it into greater action. It stampeded around the house, until it managed to dislodge the spear. Blood droplets dotted the floury floor as the pig's eyes seemed to grow red in the firelight. Lowering its tusks, the boar charged at George, only to be stopped by the wall beneath the window. George readied another spear but he only managed to jab at the pig before it darted away with an angry squeal. Melitta couldn't even tell if he'd wounded it this time.

What followed, Melitta could only call a battle of wills between Sir George and the beast. The beast would charge George, George would attempt to stab it with a spear, sometimes successfully, sometimes not. Then the beast would retreat, only to charge George again. Minutes passed, or maybe it was hours. Melitta could not be sure. Finally she was left holding the last spear. The others lay splintered inside the bakery, except for the one George still held his hand. The boar disappeared into the fog of smoke and flour, so that this time when it charged, it surprised Melitta. Yet something in her refused to just sit and watch this time. With George square in front of the window, she couldn't line up a perfect shot with the beast's chest, but she could at least do some damage, she decided.

Tightening her grip on the spear, she offered up a prayer to anyone who was listening: Let this battle end now.

George's spear struck it in the chest, and the boar lifted its head to let out a screech of pain.

Melitta took her chance, burying the point of her spear in the soft flesh at its throat. The boar backed up, tearing the spear from its flesh even as it ripped the weapon out of her hand. A gout of blood erupted into a crimson waterfall that turned the white flour into red mud. The beast tottered for a moment, as if drunk on the cider Melitta had denied it, before it collapsed for the final time.

"We did it," she said, surprised at how shaky her voice sounded. Heroes should have steadier voices, so she tried again. "We did it." There, that was better.

"I'd say that you have," a deep voice said behind her.

Melitta whirled. Somehow, while the battle had raged, the entire town had assembled behind them, and the dawn lit up their distinctly unfriendly faces.

"You destroyed the only bakery in town, and my house," the baker continued.

George drew himself up. "Your boar did that, not us," he said. "If we hadn't stopped him, he might've rampaged through your town. Who knows how much more damage he would have caused?"

A hard-eyed woman stepped forward. "That beast never attacked buildings, just people. And where will I get my bread tomorrow, now? All the dough was trampled in the dirt." She pointed at George's feet.

Only now did Melitta realise that George must have swept the bread dough off the windowsill when he dived out of the bakery.

"We'll pay for the bread out of our reward," George began.

The baker turned red. "Your reward won't even pay for half of the flour that beast destroyed. Seems to me you should be paying the town for the damage you caused. You're worse than any pig."

Melitta bit her lip, knowing before she did what she would read in the minds of the townsfolk. They had to get out of there, and fast.

"We should go," she murmured to George, tugging urgently at his arm.

He glanced at her, then said, "We'll just get out things and our horses and be on our way then." He made as if to march through the crowd to the inn.

The townspeople were having none of it. They close ranks, barring his way, and it all went downhill from there.

Fifteen

"Run!" Melitta screamed.

George's feet weren't stupid – they obeyed. His head took a moment to catch up, by which time he'd drawn level with Melitta. "We should get our things, and our horses," he gasped out.

She shook her head. "They wanted to lynch us. My horse and a few clothes aren't worth dying for."

George opened his mouth to ask how she knew that. They'd seemed like reasonable townspeople. Surely, he could talk them around to giving them at least some of the reward they'd promised…

"No. That baker is the most influential man in the village, the one putting up most of the reward, and he wanted us quartered. He'd seen it done once to a traitor when he was a boy, and he longed to see it done again. His memories are quite gruesome, and his imagination…even more so. Especially when he was imagining me getting quartered." Melitta screwed up her face, then tapped her head. "Mind-reader, remember? For my sins."

George swallowed, then accelerated. Being roasted by a dragon was one thing, but dying at the hands of a mob? That was no fitting end for a hero.

They ran until every breath burned in George's chest, but he didn't stop. He didn't dare look behind him, either, for he knew it would only slow him down.

He started to feel lightheaded, and he nearly cried when Melitta said, "They're gone. No one's close enough to hear any more. We can…stop."

She sank to her knees, her chest heaving as she gasped for breath.

George slowed, his eyes fixed on her breasts. Would they heave like that if he kissed her?

Melitta drew a dagger from her belt and waved it in his direction. "Touch me and I'll cut you."

Right. Mind-reader. How could he forget? George swallowed and fought to turn his thoughts to more practical matters. Like where he could lie down and not move for a few hours, without being disturbed.

He stumbled along the road a way, before he found what he wanted – a trail that led to a small clearing, with the remains of a long-dead fire in the middle. "We'll camp here for the night," he called.

Melitta staggered through the trees. "I'm camping here for the day. You might have slept last night, but I didn't." She settled herself on a patch of pine needles, wrapped her cloak around her, and dropped almost immediately into slumber.

George's reasonable mind reminded him that someone should stay awake to keep watch, but he was too tired to care. If he was truly in trouble, his fairy godmother would save him. Or if Lady Zoraida wouldn't, then Melitta's godmother would come.

He found a patch of grass that was reasonably flat, stretched out and prayed that things would look better when he awoke.

Sixteen

Hunger woke Melitta. She stretched, stiff from sleeping on the ground, but she'd been too tired to care. Judging by the light, it was mid-afternoon – she'd slept half the day. Not nearly long enough, but she was too hungry to stay asleep. What she wouldn't give for a plate of stew like she'd eaten last night. Or a chunk of roasted boar…

She'd killed the beast. King Erik had always made a point of offering the first morsel of meat to the hunter who landed the killing blow at hunt feasts. Those townspeople owed her that much. Ungrateful peasants.

"Sir George," she called, softly at first, then a little louder, until the cloak-shrouded form on the grass shifted.

"Mmph?"

"Sir George, perhaps we should seek out an inn, for a bed and a meal. Where are we headed next?"

George sat up and glared at her. "And pay for it with what? Do you have any money on you to pay for room and board? Mine is in my saddlebags, in the stable with the horse you insisted we leave behind."

Melitta's mouth dropped open. No money? No…meal?

"But they were going to kill us," she said.

George snorted. "So you say. But what do I have except your word for it? If you read minds so well, what am I thinking about now?" He closed his eyes and bared his teeth.

Melitta swallowed, then bit her lip to read his thoughts. "You're…you're thinking it's my fault we're out here with no money and no horses. If I'd trapped the boar properly, none of this would have happened." For a moment, her heart constricted in her chest. He was right. If the boar had stayed in the trap instead of escaping…

She'd heard the latch click shut.

Melitta jumped to her feet. "I shut that gate. You must have opened it when you leaned on it to throw your spear. Or the pig burst it open when it charged. At you. This isn't my fault. This is yours. And what kind of hero runs away, anyway? If you hadn't run, it wouldn't have chased you. You're a coward, Sir George. You don't deserve to be a knight!"

George winced. "I'm not."

"You are a coward! I saw you! I killed the beast, not you! You couldn't even stab it properly when you had it penned in the bakery!"

George rose. "I'm not a knight."

Melitta couldn't seem to find the words to respond. Finally, she managed to say, "What are you, then?"

"A hero who wants to slay a dragon."

Her mind whirled. "You mean you've never slayed a dragon before? What did you do, run away from that, too?"

George bowed his head. Melitta didn't need to read his mind to know what that meant.

"Coward! Lying, cheating coward! You said you wanted to train me to be a hero, when you wouldn't know a hero if one danced naked before you. I'm more of a hero than you'll ever be. At least I slayed that boar!"

"And a dozen with one blow before that, in case I forget," George muttered.

The taunt barely stung, coming from him.

"I demand you take me home," Melitta insisted.

George spread his arms wide. "I'm not stopping you."

Melitta set her hands on her hips. "A lady must have an escort. An armed escort. You might not be a knight, but I am the daughter of one. The daughter of a knight and his lady, and a lady of Queen Margareta's court, no less."

George's breath hissed out through his teeth. "A lady? Are you serious? A lady who ran away from court to chase dragons? I'm surprised we made it this far without your knightly father coming to drag you back home. He should be along before nightfall, if we're lucky."

"He's dead. He died defending the convent where I was born. He's a saint now," Melitta said.

George sketched a sweeping bow. "My condolences, then."

"My lady." Melitta said through gritted teeth.

"What?"

"My lady. You might not be a knight, or any kind of nobility, but you will address me properly," Melitta replied.

George unfastened a pouch from his belt and tossed it to her. "Well, then, my lady, how about you start a fire and start making us something to eat, while I go get some more firewood for tonight. Because if your saintly father isn't going to come riding in here on his heavenly steed, this is where we're camping. In case you didn't notice, we took the south road out of town, and no one else has passed this way all day. Unusual, given it's usually such a busy trade route between the town and the sea. The next inn is a day's ride, or several days on foot, but that's the least of our worries. This road is rumoured to be home to a particularly nasty band of bandits with considerable bounties on their heads. They may or may not be giants, according to some of the stories."

"Giants." Melitta couldn't keep the disbelief out of her tone. "Everyone knows there's no such thing as giants."

"People say the same about dragons. Do you believe in those?"

Suddenly, Melitta wasn't sure. If George had lied about being a hero who could teach her things, had he lied about the dragon, too?

"Maybe?" she ventured.

He nodded slowly. "That's fair. Until I saw the beast with my own eyes, even I couldn't be sure. I may not be a knight, or any kind of hero of reknown, but I swear I will kill that dragon. And if you stick with me, I'll show the beast to you."

Melitta curled her lip in disgust. "Why would I stick with you at all?"

George's smile was grim. "Bandits, remember? Even if they aren't giants, two against a band is better odds than one girl with a dagger."

Despite herself, Melitta shivered. She didn't want to admit it, but he was right. "Fine."

"I'll be back soon, then," he said, striding through the trees.

"Wait, where are you going?"

He stopped. "To get firewood, of course. While you start a fire and make a start on the evening meal. Can you handle that, my lady? Or will you need servants to do it for you?"

"I was raised in a convent before my mother and I came to court. We all had chores to do.

I'm not some useless princess, you know. In case you forgot, I killed that boar."

George inclined his head. "So you did. Maybe you can use your skills to catch us something smaller for supper." And with that, he vanished into the forest.

Melitta swallowed. Even if there were bandits on this road, it wasn't like they had anything to steal, she consoled herself as she set about finding some kindling for the fire.

Seventeen

She was a lady. A court lady, no less. So far out of his reach she might as well be a princess, George fumed as he marched down the road. A lady with a fairy godmother, even. He should have guessed from the cut of her clothes when they first met. But he'd been so mesmerised by the thought of a woman warrior, a girl with the courage he lacked, he hadn't noticed…

She'd dealt the death blow to that boar, and no mistake. She hadn't hesitated at all — one stroke, one shot, and the deed was done. For all his fumblings with the other spears, she'd made him look like a callow boy. She'd hunted with royalty – that pig couldn't have been her first kill.

He was so stupid!

What he should be thinking about was how to find firewood in a forest. Oh, sure, there was wood aplenty, but it was all part of trees that would need several well-placed blows with an axe George did not have before they'd part with anything resembling firewood. Perhaps a tree or branch that had fallen…

But this patch of forest seemed far too clean, even for George's town-bred eyes. Surely there should be more branches on the ground, yet there were none. Almost as though the undergrowth had been picked clean of fire fuel by too many travellers, or a nearby town or…a large band of bandits.

George almost laughed at himself. He'd only heard about the bandits because there was a reward for their heads, but the descriptions of them varied so much, it was hard to know what to believe. A large band, or giants…evidently they'd attacked some knight or other who'd spread the story of them being such a formidable foe. It was probably one man with a crossbow.

Finally, he spotted what he sought – a freshly fallen tree, lying across the road. Better yet, embedded in the stump was an axe. Uttering a grateful prayer of thanks, George wrapped his fingers around the haft and tugged on the weapon. It didn't budge.

Deep, booming laughter echoed through the trees, and George's heart sank. A man clad in shaggy furs that blended in with the bark of the tree behind him unfolded to a height George had to admit made him quite the giant.

Perhaps the rumours were true, he thought uneasily, before he banished that thought.

"You're not strong enough, boy," the man said, prying the axe from the stump with one hand. "See? Takes a proper man to wield such a weapon."

George's feet wanted to run, and he was ready to let them do as they pleased, but he had nowhere to run except back to Melitta. A lady who would be quite the prize to a bandit like this one. George's blood ran cold. Would he sell her as a slave, or use her as one? Or both?

He might not be a knight, but he was all the protector she had. He couldn't lead this man to her.

George forced himself to shrug and feign nonchalance. "I prefer a sword or a spear, mostly. Better for slaying dragons and other such beasts. Trees don't exactly put up much of a fight, do they? Less of a challenge."

The man tossed the axe at George's feet, where it stuck in the earth, inches from his toes. "Go ahead, boy. If you can cut through the trunk, you can have a seat at my fire tonight."

George thought quickly. "Why cut it up here? Why not just take the whole tree to your fire and cut it close to where you need it? I'll help you carry it instead. It seems only fair if I share your fire." And it would keep the man far from Melitta.

"You think you can carry half of this, boy?" The man grunted as he hefted the trunk onto his shoulder.

George eyed the tree. "Sure. The branches and leaves are much bigger than the trunk, after all. But you'll have to lift your end a little higher, or the branches will drag on the ground and slow us both down. I'm plenty strong, though I'm not as tall as you."

With what looked like considerable effort, the man tilted the tree so the branches cleared the ground. George buried his hands in the branches without taking any of the tree's weight. "Great, that's great. Lead the way!"

The giant glanced back, but most of George was hidden behind the tree, so there wasn't much for the man to see. With another grunt, he set off down the road. Away from Melitta.

With his hands full of leaves, George followed in the man's wake. He prayed fervently that he was doing the right thing, because he was damned if he knew what that was right now.

Eighteen

In nearly no time at all, Melitta had a small fire burning in the clearing. Supper, however, would be another matter. When she dug into the pouch George had given her, she found nothing but a few crumbs and a piece of cheese that looked like it had seen better days.

Like he'd said, if she wanted supper, she'd have to catch it herself.

Armed with only a dagger, she doubted she'd catch anything worth eating, if she even knew where to look.

She thought hard, remembering the times she'd gone hunting with the queen. The hunt she'd enjoyed most had been at a large lake where the river curved, and many birds congregated in the winter time. They'd shot so many, the whole court had feasted on goose for weeks. Queen Margareta had commented that hunting on the water hardly seemed fair, for every animal must drink and the hunters had so many advantages.

Melitta must find water, then, she decided. Both to drink, and to hunt. And water ran downhill, so all she had to do was head down, and she should find some. Satisfied with her logic, she set off in search of a stream.

Twice she considered turning back, but the second time, she thought she heard running water. Instead of stopping, this spurred her on, until Melitta splashed into a tiny stream. The rivulet was scarcely large enough to do more than wet her boots, but she followed it until she came to its end in what at first appeared to be little more than a puddle. Melitta parted the bushes and found herself ankle deep in a lake that stretched more than a hundred yards across. And on the edges, standing in the shallows, was a veritable badelynge of ducks.

Her heart soared, then sank to the very depths of the lake as she realised she had no way of catching any of them. Short of leaping on top of one and cutting its throat, which would surely frighten them all off. She'd end up covered in mud for the price of one bird, if she even managed to catch it.

No, there must be a better way.

The boys in the town outside the convent had occasionally brought birds to sell. Without shoes or weapons, she'd wondered how they managed to catch them. When she'd asked, one boy had showed her his slingshot. They'd thrown stones at the birds eating the grain in the fields, Melitta remembered now. The sisters had always bought the birds and baked them into big pies, sometimes even for the Harvest Feast.

The ducks were bigger than the boys' birds,

but they should still fall to a well-placed stone. Melitta hunted along the lakeshore for suitable stones, tucking them into the pouch at her waist. When she had filled the pouch, Melitta crouched behind a bush, trying to decide which duck to target first.

That one. It looked plumper than the others – if she scared the rest away when she killed it, that one duck alone would make a suitable meal.

She grasped a stone and drew her hand back, ready to throw.

Without warning, the entire flock took flight, quacking and flapping in panic for no reason Melitta could see.

Melitta swore. Then she glimpsed movement out of the corner of her eye, and slowly turned.

The source of the panic stood calmly on the branch of a dead tree at the water's edge, clutching its dinner in one talon. The falcon might have been the twin of Queen Margareta's favourite hunting bird, but this magnificent creature wore no jesses. It was as free as the sky above, and judging from the tilt of its proud head, sovereign of all it surveyed.

"You cost me my dinner, bird," she muttered, sending the rock in his direction instead. Her missile fell woefully short, splashing into the water three yards from the tree.

Melitta tried again, and again. Each time she got closer, until finally one stone hit the branch beside the falcon. It spread its wings and took off, letting its prey fall as it flew away.

Without thinking, Melitta ran for the creature the falcon had caught, hoping it would be something suitable for her own dinner. She picked up the tiny bird, so small it fitted into her hand, and almost laughed. She'd seen bigger mice in the castle at home.

But as she scooped the bird up, she felt the thrumming of its terrified heart. It was still alive.

She lifted it higher so that she might inspect it, and the bird lay still as the dead on her palm, frozen in fright.

"So you frightened away my dinner!" a voice boomed over the water as a man strode into view. "Maybe I'll eat you instead." He laughed.

Melitta tucked the bird into her now-empty pouch, and planted her feet firmly. She was tired, she probably looked like she'd been sleeping in the woods, and she was hungrier than ever, but she'd be damned before she showed fear to a man who looked wilder than she. Why, his bramble-bush beard looked like it hadn't been trimmed in months, if at all, and his clothes looked they'd last been worn by a bear. But he had a bow and a quiver full of arrows, not to mention the huge sword sheathed at his side.

"It wasn't me," she returned, tossing her head. "A falcon made the ducks take fright. He stole my dinner as much as he stole yours."

He scooped up a stone and advanced on her. "I saw you throwing rocks, girl. Do you know what I do to those who defy me? I crush them, like this." To Melitta's horrified fascination, he squeezed his fist and when he opened it, nothing but dust flew out.

Melitta gulped. She reached into her pouch, but found nothing except the bird and the piece of cheese. Clutching the cheese in her hand, she fought to keep her voice calm as she said, "Dust? That's nothing. Anyone can turn a stone to dust. I can make them weep." She clenched her fist and liquid dripped through her fingers to the ground.

This made the man hesitate. "You some kind of sorceress or something?"

"Yes, I am," Melitta said truthfully.

"How far can you and your magic throw a stone, then?" he challenged, seizing another rock which he skipped across the lake.

"Further than you," Melitta returned, uttering a silent prayer as she drew the bird from her pouch, hiding it as best she could from his watchful eyes as she launched it into the air. Either someone had heard her prayer or the bird had recovered, for once it was airborne, the bird kept flying, far away. "See?"

she said triumphantly. "I can throw a stone so far it never comes down!" She pointed to where she could barely make out the bird as a speck in the sky.

"I don't see it." The man's voice was alarmingly close. Too close.

While Melitta had been distracted, watching the bird's flight, he'd crept up behind her. She reached for her dagger, but didn't have time to pull it out before something hard crashed into the back of her head and everything went dark.

Nineteen

The first thing Melitta was aware of was the lecherous thoughts of a group of nearby men. That was hardly a surprise, though the vague inclusion of herself in those thoughts was worrying. More worrying still was the realisation that if she was reading their minds, she must have shed some of her blood. Only then did she recollect the blow to her head, which now throbbed faintly. She had been unconscious for several hours, then, she decided.

Melitta attempted to reach for the back of her head, to assess the damage, but she found that she could not. Her hands were tightly bound behind her with coarse rope. A normal girl might've panicked, but as the daughter of a master weaver who was as experienced at untangling knots as she was at breathing, Melitta simply set to work. In a moment her nimble fingers had set her free.

She sent her thoughts out to those of the unpleasant men. There were six of them, she found. All clad in fur and leather, like the clothes of raiders from the North. The man who had attacked her was among them, and she burned with anger and the desire for revenge on the man who had hit her and evidently carried her off to this place. He would pay for his disrespect. The others… Their thoughts marked them as little better than him, given what they wanted to do to her. They sat in the middle of a sort of longhouse, lounging around a fire. Though none of them was actually looking at her, she skipped through their thoughts until she found a man who was at least looking vaguely in her direction. She lay on a straw pallet in the shadows at the far end of the longhouse. She was far enough away that if she chose to, and no one saw her, she could sneak out of the place and escape. However, that left the matter of revenge.

She took a deep breath, then wished she hadn't, for the straw she lay on was far from clean. Other captives like herself had been dragged here, she realised, and forced to endure the attention of these horrible men as they slaked their lust. That hadn't been the end for the poor girls, either – after the men were done raping them, they sold the girls into slavery. Melitta's anger blazed within her. This ended here and now. They had taken their last slave.

Conversation around the fire shifted and she was surprised to see George in their thoughts. They had shared a meal with the man sometime earlier – Melitta's stomach rumbled at the thought of the meal she had missed – and he had since fallen asleep on a bed not far from where she lay.

Melitta suppressed a smile as she realised their thoughts of him were tinged with fear. Had he fooled them into thinking he was a hero of some sort, too? They seemed to think he was uncommonly strong, carrying a whole tree to their camp, when keeping up with him had almost killed one of their number. The man in question ventured that it would be safest to kill George before he woke. Several of his companions agreed.

Slowly, Melitta opened her eyes. George was indeed asleep, just where they'd thought he was, and if she kept to the shadows, she might be able to reach him without any of them seeing. He might be a charlatan and no hero at all, but he was the only ally she had against them. And he might not be a hero but he was correct when he'd said that two against a band of brigands was better than her against all six. Besides, she might not like him, but it didn't seem honourable to let these men slaughter him in his sleep.

The men began to argue loudly. Some wanted George dead, and some feared to do the deed. Those whose voices roared the loudest had minds petrified by fear. While they struggled to decide whether it was more dangerous to attempt to kill George or to let him live, Melitta took her chance. Keeping close to the wooden walls of the longhouse, she made her way to the alcove where George lay. Remembering a trick the young squires in the castle played on one another, she pinched George's nostrils shut with one hand while clapping her other hand over his mouth. He woke with a start, just as the boys had. She released his nose but kept her hand over his mouth as she whispered in his ear, "They are planning to kill you. Quickly, bundle up your bedding so that it looks like you are still here asleep, and come with me." George did as she asked, then followed her to the darkest end of the longhouse. Melitta was delighted to discover that they'd ended up in the bandits' storeroom. Now, she could finally satisfy her hunger. The two-day-old bread she sank her teeth into tasted like ambrosia. And the first flagon of wine she uncorked… even better still. She stopped after a few sips, though. It would not do to dull her wits. She would need them as sharp as possible to achieve her ends before the night was over. She glanced back the way they had come to find the men's argument had erupted into blows. They could not reach agreement on whether George should live or die. What the others did not know, though, was that one man had already made up his mind. No matter what the others decided, he would make sure George didn't live to see morning.

After some time, the fighting ceased. Two of them headed off, muttering, even as they bundled themselves into bed. The remaining four sat drinking around the fire, until one by one, they succumbed to the potent brew.

All but one – the man who had vowed

George would die. He drank sparingly, and his companions were too drunk to notice. When he was certain the others were asleep, he took his axe and stumbled toward George's bed. His head was a jumble of thoughts, the uppermost of which was anger at some trick George had played on him. A trick he suspected but did not quite understand. Disliking what he didn't understand, the man took courage from this and hefted his axe.

With one terrible blow, he cleaved the bed in two. Not content with this, he chopped at the bedclothes several more times, as if to sever George's head, feet and manhood. Then, somewhat satisfied, the would-be butcher headed for his own bed, where he curled up beside his axe like a normal man might cuddle up to a lover.

When Melitta was certain they were all asleep, she whispered to George, "We should burn this place down around them while they sleep."

"No man deserves to be burned alive!" he

whispered back, his eyes wide with horror.

"They rape and kill for fun," she hissed back. "If the king's men caught them, they'd be strung up and slaughtered, like the beasts they are."

"How do you…" George swallowed, falling silent as he remembered. "Mind-reader. Right. We should take some of the food out of here first, and then barricade the doors so that they can't escape when the fire takes hold."

Melitta nodded in satisfaction. Two against six would be more than enough for this night's work.

Twenty

George and Melitta dragged barrels and bales from the longhouse, stacking them up in the clearing outside. He couldn't help darting worried glances at the bandits each time they were in view, but the thunderous snoring was oddly reassuring.

Then Melitta came out of the door, carrying a burning brand.

"We could just leave," George suggested. "Let the king's men catch up with them and administer justice."

"I won't let them rape another woman," Melitta insisted.

His blood ran cold. "Did they…?" he began, staring at her.

She glared back. "No. And if we kill them before they wake, they won't." She hefted her makeshift torch.

"You can't burn the building. It's sod. The best it will do is smoulder," George told her. He felt oddly relieved by the admission. She would have worked it out on her own, he reasoned.

She kicked a nearby crate in frustration. "Then how are we supposed to kill them and claim the bounty on their heads?"

The bounty? George felt lightheaded. They didn't stand a chance against six men, each of them easily twice his size.

Melitta wasn't paying attention to him. Instead, she fished about inside the crate she'd kicked. "Perfect," she breathed. "We'll shoot them."

"What?"

Melitta straightened, holding a crossbow in each hand. "There's a dozen of these, and quarrels, too. Load them and stack them —" she surveyed the clearing "— beside those two trees. They give a good view of the door to the longhouse. When they emerge, we'll shoot them. No need to reload if all the bows are ready to go."

George's stomach roiled. Shooting a man from an ambush hardly seemed more honourable than killing one in his sleep. "We don't need the bounty," he lied weakly.

Melitta shoved the crossbows at him. "Load them, I said. You owe me a horse. I'm not walking home," she said. She grabbed another armload of weapons and began winding the first one up. When she'd finished, she dropped the rest at his feet. "I'll light up the roof." She advanced with her brand again, touching it to the longhouse. The sod began to smoulder in places, flaring into flame where dried grass had taken root.

"It won't be enough. The smoke it outside,

not in," George told her. Though his heart rebelled against it, urging him to run, he continued loading the crossbows in accordance with her command.

Melitta frowned at the roof. "Then I'll have to go inside and light the place up. Starting with that smelly pallet." Before George could stop her or call a warning to be careful, Melitta marched back into the longhouse with murder in her eyes.

For a long moment, he waited, listening to the click of each crossbow before he set it in readiness beside its fellows. Seconds ticked by and his heart sank at the thought of having to go in after Melitta to save her. Would he be too late?

Shouldering the final crossbow, George took a step toward the door.

Melitta erupted from the longhouse, sprinting toward him. "Fire!" she cried, pointing behind her.

So she'd lit it, George thought, until he realised that wasn't what she meant at all. An angry giant of a man burst out of the door after her. George fired the crossbow. The bolt caught the man in the throat, and he collapsed on the ground with a gurgle before he lay still.

"One down, five to go," Melitta said, pointing a bow at the dark doorway. She had a smudge of soot on her cheek, but her eyes blazed with fire.

Once again, George fell in love.

"Get him!"

Melitta fired before George could even aim. Her bolt caught the man in the belly. She swore, picked up another bow, and fired again. This one penetrated his forehead, felling him like the tree George had pretended to help him carry here.

He didn't have time to reflect on it, though, for two men fought to get out of the doorway next, and they both had to choose their targets. His first shot missed both of them, to George's dismay, but the second one plunged into his quarry's thigh. Before George could fire again, Melitta's quarrel found his chest.

"Four!" she cried, reaching down for another weapon.

The fifth man charged out of the door, straight at her, bellowing, "Witch!"

Melitta dropped her bow in surprise.

Thank the heavens the man hadn't seen George, for George had scarcely a moment to bring his bow up to fire at the man before the giant reached Melitta. He wasn't fast enough to stop him, either – the man crashed into Melitta, throwing her to the ground. She managed to tug out her dagger and plunged it into his side before either of them realised he'd stopped moving. The fletching of George's bolt stuck out behind the man's ear.

Melitta rolled the man off her with difficulty. George moved to help, but she hissed, "Watch the door. There's still one left!"

The sixth man had already made it out the doorway, but instead of heading for them, he took off at a run. George didn't think. He paused only to snatch up a second bow before he was off after the man, trying to get a clear shot as the giant weaved through the trees.

As if by magic, a crossbow quarrel sprouted from the man's back, and he keeled over, face first. When George reached him, he wasn't sure if the man was alive or dead. He prodded the man's shoulder with his bow. "Get up," he said.

The man rolled, seizing George's bow in one hand and bringing a blade up with the other.

A bolt pierced the man's eye, and the knife dropped from his fingers as he fell back to the ground, lifeless.

George turned.

Melitta stood a dozen yards away, crossbow clutched to her side, with a look of grim satisfaction on her face. "He didn't deserve a quick death. None of his victims got one."

George looked askance at her, not trusting his voice. She'd killed a man. No, she'd killed four. He'd killed two. For all his talk of heroism and honour, he'd never killed a man before today.

"Not all the girls these men took were sold as slaves. This one liked to torture them, sticking knives into them so they bled to death while he raped them. He wanted to do the same to me." Melitta kicked the corpse.

George drew in a shaky breath. If she was right, these men deserved to die. Bandits, with bounties on their heads, he reminded himself. A bounty they could use to replace what they lost in Sanglier.

"See if you can find some sacks," George found himself saying.

Melitta frowned at him. "What for?"

George dropped to his knees and reached for the dead man's blade. "We'll need to put these heads in something so we can carry them to town to claim the bounty."

Now it was Melitta's turn to look sick. "Right. All right. I'll see what I can find."

Twenty-One

A tentative knock sounded at the door. Melitta crossed the inn's best chamber to open it. "Yes?" she asked.

The chambermaid dropped a curtsy. "Beg pardon, milady. I thought this was the knight's chamber."

"George's across the hall, in what I understand is your second best chamber," Melitta said, pointing. "He said that a lady deserves the best, and a knight will make do with whatever else is available."

"Aw, he's a gallant one, isn't he? All chivalry and courtly love." She sighed blissfully. "So romantic. When will you be married, milady?"

Married? Melitta's eyebrows rose so high she suspected they vanished into her hair. Hopefully never, she thought but didn't say. Instead, she replied, "When a man demonstrates he truly deserves me, and asks for my hand."

At the sound of a male voice clearing his throat, the maid turned bright red. The girl spun on the spot. "Your armour has arrived, good Sir Knight," she mumbled. She bobbed a curtsy, holding out the box. She waited only long enough for George to take it from her hands before she hurried off downstairs.

George's eyes met Melitta's. His expression was unreadable. "So do we open it in your chamber or mine? After all, one set of this armour belongs to you."

Now it was Melitta's turn to blush. If she was going home to court, she truly didn't need armour. But after killing that boar and then the giants… People looked at her differently. Well, they looked at George mostly, for he was the hero who had claimed the bounty on the bandits. But he'd split the money with her immediately, instead of taking the lion's share for himself, as Melitta would have expected. Though she might have killed more of the men, she was still just an apprentice hero.

"Mine is larger," Melitta said opening the door wider to allow George in.

He set the box on the table and pulled out the first piece of armour. Holding it up to his chest, he said, "I believe this is yours."

He was right. The leather curved in ways that no man's armour should, or needed to. Melitta felt the urge to buckle it on immediately, though there was no enemy here. She still occasionally remembered the gory mess George had made hacking off the six giants' heads, for she had been unable to hold down her gorge long enough to help. George had not complained, nor even mentioned it, for which she was grateful. She thought she should feel something, after killing those men, but if anything she was glad. Proud to have been the one who stopped them from hurting anyone else. Was this what George had first seen in her on the day they met? The makings of a true hero?

She watched him buckle his own armour over his tunic, as eager as she was to see how well it fit. He'd chosen leather, like her, despite the reward being enough for them to afford steel. Not to mention all the goods the bandits had stolen, which by right of conquest had belonged to both of them after the men were dead. She knew George still carried some of the jewels in the bottom of his saddlebags — insurance against the day when he might need to sell them. For a gold necklace could buy a fine horse and enough food to keep a hero going until his next quest. He'd offered some to her, but she had refused. When would she ever wear them? She'd left all her jewels back in her mother's apartments in the castle. She had no need for more.

"I took the liberty of ordering you new boots as well," George said, pulling a pair out of the box. "Yours appear to have been damaged by water at some point."

Though it seemed such a long time ago now, Melitta remembered the exact moment when it happened. She'd gotten her feet wet collecting stones to catch birds for their dinner on the lake, and all the trouble of being captured by giants and fighting her way free, she hadn't noticed they were ruined until too late. "Thank you," she said.

He cleared his throat. "If you'll allow me, I have a special potion of my own design, that when rubbed on shoes properly can make them entirely waterproof. I can do it tonight, and then you never need worry about getting your feet wet, ever again." He shuffled his own feet on the floor boards, keeping his head down and not meeting her eyes.

"I would be very grateful," Melitta said truthfully. "Wherever did you find such a magical potion?"

George laughed. "In my father's workshop. He was a shoemaker, and until I chose a different path, so was I. His creations were much sought after at court, as were my mother's. Her embellishments were so beautiful, she made boots for the king and queen themselves. My work… was of a more practical bent. I was never as good as my father, or my mother. So I made shoes for the rest of the town, while my mother and father made shoes for those who could afford the best."

Melitta touched the leather. "So did you make these, or someone else?" They were as fine as any she'd worn at home, but her knowledge was all about cloth, not leather.

George smiled sadly. "Not me. You deserve the best, so a better shoemaker than me made them. Perhaps not as fine as my mother's work, but she had a rare gift, may God rest her soul." He spread his hands wide. "May I help you put them on, to see if they fit?"

Melitta couldn't say no. She perched on the

edge of a chair and George knelt before her. She held out one booted foot, which George clasped reverently. He pulled off her ruined shoe, then cupped her heel in his hand before sliding the new boot on in its place.

"Perfect," he breathed, reaching for her other foot.

He took longer with the second one, pausing to smooth her wrinkled hose.

His stroking fingers seemed to set her heart racing as Melitta's breath caught in her throat. True, no man had ever touched her feet before, but her body reacted as if this was more than just a touch. Melitta prayed he didn't notice the strange effect he had on her.

He slid the second boot on as easily as the first, then urged her to stand and walk. She obeyed, marvelling at the softness of the leather around her foot, though the sole was thicker than she was used to. More practical than what she'd worn around the castle, though of no less quality. George might not have made these boots, but he had commissioned them, and he was a good enough shoemaker to know what was best. Yes, the fit was perfect.

"Thank you," she said again, trying to emphasise how much she meant it.

"My pleasure, my lady." George clambered to his feet. "Shall I help you with your armour, too, to make sure that fits as well?"

Melitta wanted to protest that she was perfectly capable of dressing herself, but she'd never donned armour before, and George had been so familiar with his own. So, she nodded.

Together, they lifted the surprisingly heavy garment over her head and settled it around her hips. He smoothed the leather across her back as she cinched the buckle around her waist. A little too tight, she realised, as she tried and failed to reach for the shoulder straps. Melitta hurried to loosen the belt.

George's breath was warm on the back of her neck. "Allow me, my lady."

She suppressed a shiver at the sound. She wasn't cold, she wasn't afraid…so why was she reacting so strangely?

George's hands smoothed the straps over her shoulders, then, one by one, he fastened the buckles on either side of her collarbone to keep the armour in place.

"George…" Her voice sounded so breathless Melitta barely recognised it. Was it just her, or did his hands linger on her for just a moment? It was hard to tell beneath the layers of wool and leather. Perhaps it was the memory of his touch that lingered.

"Yes, my lady?" He stepped around her, then stood before her, his eyes taking in every detail. From the curve of his lips, she believed he either liked what he saw or he was trying not to laugh.

Melitta longed for a mirror, but even the best room in the inn had no such luxury. So, she did as she always had on such occasions — she bit her lip and slipped into someone else's eyes to see what she looked like.

Warmth engulfed her, as passionate as a lover's embrace. "A true goddess, a goddess of war," George's voice rumbled, though his lips never moved. In that moment, Melitta felt like the most beautiful woman she'd ever seen, and loved like…like the way King Erik worshipped his queen.

Gasping, Melitta withdrew back into her own head, grasping the table to stop herself from stumbling over her own feet. Some goddess, she thought angrily. "What do you think?" she asked George.

Adoration still warmed his eyes, but his tone was more businesslike than his thoughts. "It fits," he said. "What does it feel like?"

Like she wanted to throw her arms around him and kiss him, Melitta thought. No, those were his thoughts, not hers, she scolded herself. "It feels fine," she said.

His expression softened, as though he could read her mind and the stray thoughts she struggled to suppress. "You look very fine."

Melitta's mouth was dry as she once again found it hard to breathe. The armour, her fuzzy mind told her. It must still be fastened too tight. If she unbuckled it, then she wouldn't feel so lightheaded. Or hot. Yes, she was too hot in all these clothes. They must come off.

Her mind slipped effortlessly into George's head, and his thoughts echoed hers. Clothes. Off. Certainly…

Twenty-Two

George couldn't tear his eyes away from her. Every fibre in his body wanted him to dart forward and take Melitta in his arms. He couldn't be imagining the invitation in her eyes.

Except…his brain refused to let him. She was Lady Melitta, companion to a queen, and he was…little more than a cobbler. Which meant he must be daydreaming.

"Milady? Sir Knight?" A maidservant dropped a deep curtsey in the doorway.

"There's a young priest downstairs, seeking the hero who killed them robbers on the coast road. He's fair wild about it, too. Says he won't eat or drink or rest until he's spoken to you." She looked at George.

He wanted to tell her she had the wrong person, and it was Milady the priest wanted, for the most he'd done was butcher the robbers' bodies for their heads and then collect the bounty for his bag of grisly remains, but he needed to escape from her chamber before temptation won him over and he did something stupid.

The lady who'd killed a dozen with one blow would end him just as easily as any of the giants. She truly was some ancient goddess of war, come to earth to…well, what she'd come for, he wasn't sure. But she'd already conquered his heart, and many men would follow.

George nodded, then followed the maid downstairs. A woman's light tread behind him told him Melitta had followed, and why not?

George could no more stop her than he could prevent the sun from rising.

The priest was a beanpole of a man who didn't look much older than George himself, yet his slumped shoulders and cavernous eyes spoke of troubles he'd endured that no many should be subject to.

"What troubles you, Father?" George asked.

The priest's eyes drank him in like a thirsty man's first gulp of water, before spitting him out again as he realised his saviour was a mirage. "Nothing and no one can help me," the priest said. "Unless I can find a man who slays monsters no one else can touch."

"Valiant Sir George here slayed a dozen giants. Cut their heads off with his sword," the maid said proudly, as though she had witnessed this remarkable feat. "He's the man you want, Father."

The priest's eyes widened. "You?"

George couldn't blame him. He knew he hardly looked like a hero. The sort of knight a lady like Melitta might look on with love. He sighed. "Two. I killed two giants. Not twelve." And, as honesty had truly taken hold of him, he added, "And I took their heads off with a knife. Severing a spine is dull work for a sword."

The priest's jaw dropped. "You killed two giants with only a knife?" He swallowed, still staring at George. "Perhaps you are the hero I seek."

George inclined his head, waiting. He could hear Melitta behind him, but she didn't say a word. Probably wanting to hear what the priest had to say before deciding whether to offer her help. George wished he'd been as cautious.

"Deep in the forest, beside a lake to the west of here, there is a holy well whose water works miracles. When the Grand Master of my order heard of it, he insisted we must build an abbey to protect such a holy site. For two years, we have waited to hear tidings that the new monastery has been built, but we received no word. Finally, my superior sent me to discover what is causing the delay.

"I journeyed for days, then took ship for the coast. From there, I headed south along the coast road. Many people told me cautionary tales about giants or robbers who preyed on travellers on the coast road, but I could not turn back. I reasoned that a solo traveller under a vow of poverty would not attract the attention of robbers, and I was relieved to find I was right. I saw not a single soul on the road until I reached the road to the lake." The priest nodded his thanks as a tavern girl handed him a cup.

He drank deeply before he continued, "The lake road showed signs of recent traffic, but I followed it all the way to the water before I found a camp of men making clay bricks for the abbey. They set them out in their moulds in the sun for some time, before firing them in an oven so they are hard enough to build with. Remarkable, really. Making their own rocks, when there is not enough stone with which to build."

George waved his hand, urging the priest to

continue.

"Bricks were piled up everywhere — enough to build an abbey to rival the one where our Grand Master resides. I explained to the men who I was, and how I would like to see how their construction fared. They conferred among themselves for a moment, before one of the men drew me down to the lake's edge. He pointed across the water and told me the well was on a particular hill overlooking the lake, and that's where they'd started to build the abbey. If I wanted, I could walk around the lake to the hill and look for myself. They had bricks to make while daylight lasted, he said."

The priest sat down heavily and drained his cup. "I followed the path around the lake. The first thing I saw was more piles of bricks. More than enough to finish an abbey, so why did they need more? Still, I ascended the hill. The builders had cut into the side of the hill to dig a huge cellar — enough to hold supplies for a large community. Perhaps the Grand Master planned to move to this abbey, I thought, which was why he wanted such a grand building. The idea stayed with me until I reached the crown of the hill, where I stopped. For there was no abbey. No church, no monastery…nothing, but that cavernous cellar on one side and, half hidden in the summer grass, a low stone well on the other."

The priest shook his head, as if reliving the moment and still not believing it. "It was a hot day, and I had quite a thirst. While I may not be as holy as some, I'd like to think I am a godly man, and I was there in obedience to the wishes of my order. So I approached the well, intending to drink those most holy waters."

Melitta made an impatient sound in her throat.

The priest hung his head. "I know, mistress. I am human, and I was tempted. I will pay my penance for such presumption, I promise. I pulled up a bucket of water, and the moment the liquid touched my lips…" Here the priest's voice seemed to fail him. He swiped a hand across his brow. "I am sorry. I…"

Twenty-Three

The priest's fear was so thick Melitta could almost taste it. Cloying and bitter, yet he drank the draught because it was his duty to do so. He lived and would die for the vows he'd made to his order.

"From the trees there erupted a creature I can only describe as the wrath of God made flesh. It shone as bright as the sun, fearsome to look at, and moved nigh as fast as that very orb's rays. The thunder of its hooves would have shaken the very heavens above as it charged toward me." The priest swallowed. "I think it would have impaled me and tossed me into the well, as a warning to others who dare to take what they do not deserve. I suspect I would have deserved my fate, but I had not the faith to accept it. Weak as I was, I ran around the well and into the forest, as fast as I could, back to the brickmakers' camp. It was only when I reached the other men that I realised the beast had not followed me, and I was safe."

Even though Melitta had seen the image in the man's mind, she didn't believe it. Such creatures couldn't exist.

And if they did, what he wanted them to do sat squarely in the realms of sacrilege.

George folded his arms across his chest. Melitta had to admit that the new breastplate made him look more muscled than was actually the case. "So you want us to go to this building site of yours, and slay a beast."

The priest nodded fervently. "Oh, yes. If you will do that, I can promise you a rich reward. Not just in heaven, but here on earth, as well. My superiors gave me enough gold to hire more labourers, if that was the problem, or material if it is missing, but no amount of coin will convince workmen to build the abbey as long as it is guarded by a fearsome beast."

"We'll take the job," George said promptly before Melitta could stop him. "Will you take us to the construction camp on the morrow?"

"Of course, Sir George," the priest said warmly, sagging with relief against the bench. He glanced at Melitta. "Are you taking the lady with you, sir?"

Dread twisted in Melitta's belly. This was a bad idea, and she needed to tell George that before he committed himself, and maybe even her, to this folly.

"Of course," George said. "It's a little known piece of lore that having a virgin present can calm even the most savage beast. She is my secret weapon." He deliberately avoided meeting Melitta's gaze.

Wait until he sees what his secret weapon

will do to him the moment no one's looking, Melitta fumed. She wanted no part in this.

The priest, who had recovered his spirits remarkably quickly, called for food and drink to celebrate the bargain he and George had made.

Try as she might, Melitta couldn't seem to get George's attention long enough to warn him about what the priest wanted. After a frustrating hour, she gave up and headed upstairs to her chamber to get some sleep. She'd tell him in the morning, she decided — right before she rode off in the opposite direction. She'd had her fill of heroes and those who hired them. She'd head home and, if she still wanted to, slay monsters there.

Twenty-Four

George plied the priest with far more drink than was good for him, but even deep in his cups, the man didn't drop so much as another hint about the beast they faced, or the best way to kill it. Which was unusual in itself, he had to admit. What man was so afraid of something he refused to talk about it at all? Didn't he want it dead?

He turned to ask Melitta, for with her mind-reading magic it was possible that she had caught more from the man than he had, but he was disappointed to discover that she'd disappeared. Back to her chamber, he assumed, resting before tomorrow's journey.

Sure enough, when he'd managed to roll out of bed the following morning and drink enough to dispel his lingering hangover, he found Melitta at breakfast in the common room downstairs, wearing her breastplate and a grim expression.

"Good morning, my lady," he wished her warmly.

Melitta eyed him over her cup, drinking deeply before she replied, "No morning is good when the day must end in killing a unicorn."

George spat out a mouthful of water. "You're killing a unicorn? But those things are purity itself. Killing one would condemn you to hell for eternity. Don't do it, my lady, I beg you."

Melitta slammed her cup down on the table. "I never said I'd do it. You did, though. You promised the priest that you'd kill his unicorn.

And virgin or not, I won't help you do it. You're on your own for this one." She rose and made to leave.

If she left, he stood no chance against the dragon. Ever.

George grasped her wrist. "My lady – Melitta – please. Don't go. I need you."

Melitta wrenched free. "I'm not killing a unicorn, George."

Possibilities spiralled through his mind. Slowly, he began, "What if we don't have to? What if we just trapped it, like we did with the boar?"

Melitta snorted. "Like that worked. Or don't you remember being run out of town without our things? And I killed the beast, in case you've forgotten."

George waved away her worries. "This isn't the same thing. I'll speak to the priest before we set out. I know all he needs is to get the beast away from the building site, so it's safe to build the abbey. If we trap it, then he can do what he likes with it. We can earn our money and be on our way to fight something more deserving of death, like a dragon."

He'd sparked her interest, he knew, but he wasn't sure if it was enough.

"Imagine the tales they'll tell about us if we not only killed a dozen giants, but captured a unicorn, too," George added.

"Six, not a dozen," Melitta replied. "And you only killed two of them."

"But a unicorn…" he wheedled. "Have you ever seen a unicorn?"

She sighed. "No. If I hadn't seen one in the priest's memories yesterday, I still wouldn't believe the creature exists. And I certainly couldn't bring myself to kill one."

"A lady who has killed a dozen with one blow, and a wild boar that was terrorising a town, and four giants…my lady, if you decide something must die, may God help anyone who stands in your way." George meant every word, but he wasn't sure Melitta believed him.

A slight smile curved at her lips. "Flatterer. You make me sound so frightening, yet I suspect I will be little more than virgin bait for the beast, if anything."

George placed his hand over his heart. "I swear by my own life that I find you terrifying, my lady."

She seemed to measure him with her eyes for a long moment, before she gave a nod. He hoped he had passed her inspection. "You promised to put your magic potion on my new boots," she said.

He bowed his head. "Indeed I did. In all the excitement last night, I forgot. I will remedy that tonight, if you allow me to."

"Before we must face the unicorn, or after?"

"Before, of course. When you meet your first unicorn, you must wear your best boots."

Melitta laughed. "I must be mad, listening to you. And yet, your words have untold power. My first unicorn. I like the sound of that too much to refuse. We will go with this priest, see his unicorn, and if he still insists the beast must be killed…then we will decline the task and be on our way."

She made it sound so easy. Yet for her, it would be, George was sure of it. He swallowed his last mouthful of breakfast. "We ride."

An hour later, ride they did — but without the priest, who had claimed illness after drinking too much the previous night. He gave them directions to the lake campsite and promised he would catch up to them. Melitta waited until she was out of his earshot before expressing her doubts that he'd arrive before they'd dealt with the beast, and George had to agree.

Still, he rode to battle alongside a veritable goddess of war whose eager enthusiasm was more contagious than any plague. Oh, but what a pleasurable plague. George felt his own courage rising every time he glanced at her.

Yes, it was his courage. Nothing else, for nothing could happen between them. Fairytales were for knights and ladies and royalty. Shoemakers were never the hero who won the heart of a fair lady. One day some prince would ask for her hand and she would be someone else's lady. Never his.

George knew his place, and counted himself fortunate that today it was at her side. What more could he ask for, except victory?

Twenty-Five

By the time the lake came into view between the trees, Melitta had to admit they had a good plan. The priest had not put in an appearance, so they'd decided to trap the beast and wait for the priest to come. When he did, they would demand payment, or release the unicorn.

The brickmakers' camp was just as the priest had described it, and the men there were only too happy to direct them to the well. Melitta was tempted to walk around the lake right away, but she agreed with George that it was best to wait a day or two for the priest to catch up to them. Surely he couldn't be more than a day behind.

On the morrow, George told the men, he would save them from the unicorn. Cheers erupted and the labourers broke out a barrel of mead they'd been saving for a special occasion. Melitta didn't tell George they believed it would be his last night alive, for they'd seen the unicorn kill several of their number before they'd retreated to the other side of the lake. Much like the boar, when it attacked, it lowered its head and charged with its horn first, attempting to impale or gore its target.

For the first time, Melitta wondered if their plan could work. She'd counted on the unicorn being a sort of skittish horse, not some fully armed, more deadly version of one of King Erik's war destriers. If one attacked her, she would most certainly fight back to protect her own life, purity be damned. How pure could a murderous beast be, anyhow?

Something to worry about in the morning,

she told herself, as she rolled herself in her cloak by the fire. The men had offered them space in the hut they shared, but Melitta had declined the offer. With that many men in a confined space all night, the smell would be unbearable.

George slept on the other side of the fire, apparently not bothered at all by what awaited them on the morrow. He was a strange man, confident as the finest knight at one moment, and as humble as the lowest servant the next.

"You should rest, my lady," he said softly.

So he wasn't asleep after all.

Melitta squinted at him through the flames. "How did you know I wasn't asleep yet?"

He chuckled. "The lining of your cloak is silk, and it rustles when you move. When you are restless, it sounds like wind rustling through the leaves above. Sleep, my lady. Tomorrow will come whether you are awake to greet it or not, and our fate is already written. You won't change the outcome of tomorrow's battle by worrying over it."

"You're not worried about dying tomorrow? If we do something wrong?"

"Tomorrow, anything could happen. We could live or die. Take a wound, catch the plague, step on a snake, be crushed by a horse, be hit by a falling tree…and die. Life is short but precious. Tomorrow, your day will end in you seeing a unicorn for the first time. Whatever else happens…is already ordained."

Melitta frowned. "I don't believe that. We have free will. We can make our own fate. I left the castle. You left your shoemaking shop. You can't know what will happen tomorrow, or what choices we will make."

"Worrying about it won't change that."

"You'd make a good court philosopher, George. Have you ever considered that?"

George snorted. "Me, at court? Surely you jest. That's your place, my lady, not mine." He sounded so sad as he said it, too. Almost as though he wished…

"Good night, George," she said.

"And sweet dreams to you, my lady."

My lady. There was something in those words, and the way he said it. Part mockery, part respect, and a lot of longing.

She'd miss that when they parted ways. But not yet. They had a unicorn to face on the morrow, and all else paled into insignificance before it.

$$\mathcal{T}\textit{wenty-}\mathcal{S}\textit{ix}$$

The men making bricks wished them luck as George and Melitta set off around the lake for the construction site. Melitta was unusually quiet, her eyes darting around as though searching for something. Perhaps she expected the unicorn to pop out of the trees to surprise her.

Did she know something about unicorns that he did not?

Probably. She seemed to know a lot about a lot of things, which constantly surprised him.

He'd thought that court ladies spent all of their time drinking, talking, and perhaps sewing. Certainly nothing particularly useful. Maybe Melitta was different, or maybe he'd just been wrong. Yet if she had fit in so well in court, what was she doing out here with him? Unless the goddess of war was lying about running away from a marriage that her parents had arranged for her, she was here because she wanted to be.

Because she wanted to be with him, a tiny voice inside his head taunted him..

Impossible. Georgie knew the score. It was a unicorn she wanted, not him. After all, she was by his side, not sparing him a glance, whilst she strained her eyes searching for the elusive beast.

The abbey was almost exactly as the priest had described it. A brick cellar carved into the cleared hillside, with the hill itself crowned by a circlet of stone that George took to be the well fed by a miraculous spring, or whatever it was. Magical, miraculous, blessed by a saint…the priest hadn't been too clear about that. All he had said was that the well had the power to heal the sick.

Now, George believed in miracles as much as the next man, but most wells that worked miracles that he had heard of worked their magic through the cleanliness of the water. No more magic required. In a city, clean water might be in short supply. Yet here, with such a large lake on their doorstep, why one would go to the trouble of digging a well for water...perhaps there was something to the stories, after all.

Not that George had any intention of needing the healing waters from the well. Together, he and Melitta would trap the unicorn, then return to camp and claim the reward when the priest arrived.

When Melitta reached the crown of the hill, she stopped. Turning around to look back the way that she'd come, a smile lit her face as she took in the view. "It's so beautiful," she breathed. "The view across the lake and over the forest… Though I would never join a religious community, I could live here."

"Why not? Are you not pious enough?" George teased.

Melitta closed her eyes and shook her head. "I grew up in a convent, remember? I know what life in the cloister is like. Reporting to the chapter house every morning for your chores, and then again every evening to report that they were done. It is all work and prayer and drudgery. Some found joy in it, but not I. Being closed within walls like that, even if you could see out… It was like being in a prison, or a tomb. I wish to live in the world, not separate from it."

"So this is what the unicorn is fighting to protect? The freedom of this hill in the forest? A domain without walls?" George asked.

Melitta shrugged. "I do not know. If the unicorn were here, perhaps I could read its mind. But as it is not, its motivation shall remain a mystery."

No unicorn? Now it was George's turn to

scan their surroundings. Of course, she was right. There was no sign of the beast. Merely the grassy rise, and the big brick pit.

"Can you do that? Read the minds of animals, I mean?" George asked.

"Sometimes. When they use natural instinct, often there are no thoughts to read. A hunting beast usually only knows hunger, and a hunted beast only knows fear. They do not wonder, 'What if?'" Melitta managed a small smile. "Perhaps they all subscribe to the philosophy you described last night. They do not worry, and so they sleep better for it."

George peered into the cellar. It certainly looked big enough for their needs. But it was deeper than he'd thought. The fall from the top might kill a man, or a beast...

"Do you think our plan will work?" George asked abruptly. A sudden thought struck him, and he glanced around again, worried. "Perhaps we'd best not talk of it. After all, a unicorn is a kind of horse and horses understand what we say. So if the beast heard us, and knew our plan, it might also be smart enough to avoid it."

"The beast is not close enough to hear us," Melitta stated with all the confidence of a woman who knew she was talking about. "Perhaps there is something we must do to summon it. What did the priest do? Drink the water from the well?" She moved toward the well, her head darting around like a bird's at every step.

George's heart rose into his throat. He would not place her in danger. Not again. "No, I should do that," he said. "I did not mean that bit about you being virgin bait. I know you're a better marksman than me, so if anyone should be the bait, it is myself." He managed a sickly smile. "If you save me from the beast, I will make shoes for you for the rest of your life."

Melitta tilted her head to the side, as if considering his offer. "Very well," she said slowly. "You draw some water. I shall stand back, and we shall see whether there is any truth to this nonsense about unicorns preferring virgins."

Her eyes glinted with mischief, and for the first time George doubted. He'd believed her to be a virtuous lady, but he'd heard talk of something called courtly love. He'd dismissed it as mere wind – sonnets and other words and such, expressing ideas and ideals that had little to do with the reality of marriage.

Another thought struck him. What if that was what Melitta had run away from? A man at court who had forced her against her will, dishonoured her, and that was why she had been so adamant that the giants must die. Anger burned in his breast. When he escorted her home, he would ask the name of the vile wretch. George might not be a knight, but he had honour, and her honour would not be satisfied until the man had breathed his last.

Melitta was laughing softly. "I meant you, you fool. No man would dare touch one of the ladies of Queen Margareta's court without the lady's permission. The queen would castrate him, before subjecting him to a slow and painful death that he justly deserved. I am as chaste as I choose to be. If the beast does not attack you, then we shall know that unicorns have a fondness for virgins. For you are one, are you not?"

Oh, by all that was holy… George's cheeks grew hot as he blushed like a maiden. Though he longed to tell her she was correct, he refused to lie to her. "I am not," he said shortly. "So the beast will react to me as savagely as he did to the priest. May your purity keep you safe."

He unhooked the bucket from the side of the well, check to make sure it was firmly tied to the coiled rope, then flung the pail into the depths. A splash sounded deep below, and George grasped the rope to haul it up once more.

Melitta's voice was scarcely more than a whisper. "George."

He continued hauling up the bucket, but his eyes were no longer on the dark depths. It seemed just a shimmer between the trees, but it rippled, moving faster than anything he'd seen. Then the horse stepped out of the trees, and George could only stare. The rope fell from his fingers, as he took in the legendary steed.

He had never seen a finer piece of horse flesh. This beast belonged in a king's stable, at the very least. Or an emperor's, perhaps. Yet when the animal raised his head, and with it the wickedly sharp horn that was easily the length of George's forearm, George knew this beast belonged in no stable in heaven or on earth.

The unicorn tossed its head in apparent agreement, before it pawed the ground.

George tensed. Now he would live, or he would die. He prayed that the plan would work. Or that Melitta would succeed when he…

The beast started forward and George bolted. He darted this way, and then that, knowing that to run in a straight line would be to court death. Death by impalement. He circled the well. Once. Twice. On the third time, he broke and ran, heading downhill in the way they'd decided.

The unicorn's hooves thundered behind him. So close. But if George turned to see how close, he would die.

Five more steps. Four. Three. George uttered a prayer. A wordless cry that this would work. Two. One.

George closed his eyes and leaped into nothingness.

Twenty-Seven

Melitta's breath caught in her throat as George jumped into the cellar. She was so certain he'd fall to his death but he managed to catch onto the opposite wall, sliding down it to the earth floor, apparently unharmed.

Melitta breathed again.

The unicorn reached the edge of the pit and it appeared to hesitate, perhaps sharing Melitta's doubts that it would survive the jump. Then it reached the same conclusion Melitta had – if the man could walk around after jumping in there, then he would be fine.

The beast backed up a few paces, then bunched its muscles and leaped.

Right at George.

Melitta screamed out a warning.

He scrambled up the wall like a monkey, digging his hands into the mortar like his life depended on it. Which perhaps it did, for if the unicorn charged at him in the confined space of the cellar, it could still kill him.

Without thinking, Melitta knelt by the lip of the hole, reaching down to help him up. Together, they dragged him over the edge and lay on the grass, gasping.

Below, the unicorn let out an angry scream like no horse Melitta had ever heard before.

George rose to his knees. "It worked," he marvelled. "The beast is trapped, just like we planned it." He beamed at her, eyes shining with relief. "And I'm still alive!"

Confident one moment, as humble as dirt the next, Melitta reminded herself. No, she'd never met a man like George before, and she probably never would again.

He leaped to his feet. "I should go and see if the priest has arrived. And tell him his abbey is safe." He offered Melitta his hand.

She declined. "I'll stay here and make sure the unicorn doesn't escape." And as she watched, she would fix every detail in her mind for later, because she doubted she'd ever see another unicorn.

George hesitated for a moment, before he came to a decision. "All right. If the priest doesn't arrive before the midday meal, I'll return with some food for you."

"Wait." Melitta held up her hand, bit her lip, and reached with her mind. She found the brick makers on the very edge of her awareness, on the other side of the lake. Most of their minds were intent on the clay they worked with, or irritated that some beast had stepped in the moulds before the clay was properly dry. But one mind bubbled with anticipation, half hoping and yet not daring to hope that George would succeed. The priest.

Melitta withdrew. It took a moment for her vision to clear, so she shook her head a few times before she said, "He's there. I can feel him."

George sighed in relief. "Then I will bring him and your midday meal."

Melitta nodded and waited for George to be on his way before she clambered to her feet. Sleeping on the ground was not the most comfortable thing she'd ever done, as her aching body chose to remind her. If she returned home after this, at least there would be soft beds every night.

But a night's discomfort was worth it to see a unicorn, Melitta reflected as she peered down at the beast. It hadn't moved from the spot where it had landed.

It raised its head and let out another horrible, almost human scream.

"I don't like walls, either," she told the animal, "but George will be back soon with that priest. He'll release you, one way or another. Just be patient."

The unicorn let out a huffy snort, just like any normal, impatient horse.

Melitta moved higher up the hill, so that she could lean against one of the few remaining trees that gave her a good vantage point from which she could watch the beast in the cellar. Of course, the view of the lake was beautiful, too, reflecting the blue sky above. Almost as pretty as the ocean at home on a clear day.

The sound of hoofs pounding on turf dragged her out of her daydream. Melitta watched in frozen horror as the unicorn, which had somehow miraculously escaped from the cellar, charged up the hill right for her.

Twenty-Eight

At first, when George told the priest they'd captured the unicorn, he'd been excited. Almost as eager as George to go back and get Melitta. But when George told him the tale of how he had trapped the beast, which was still alive, the priest's enthusiasm waned significantly.

First, he had to see to his horse: make sure the beast was fed and brushed and tethered so that it could not escape. Then he needed to change out of his travelling clothes, for such dusty garments were disrespectful to wear when visiting such a holy site. Then, he needed to relieve himself, which took an inordinately long amount of time, at least in George's opinion.

Finally, when the priest appeared to be ready, George told him of his promise to bring a midday meal for Melitta. The priest's eyes lit up at this, as he busied himself putting together a veritable feast for the three of them to share on the hilltop.

Privately wondering how they were supposed to carry so much food, let alone eat it, George set off around the lake again, with the priest staggering along behind him.

Urgency quickened George's steps, though he did not understand why. Melitta was more than capable of defending herself, and there was no way the unicorn could get out of the cellar. George himself had struggled to climb the wall. A beast with hooves and no hands stood no chance. Yet still he worried, and wondered why.

If the priest's far-off abbey knew of the miraculous properties of the well water, then plenty of others must know of it, too. At any time, a knight might come on the quest for the water and if such a man found Melitta at the well…who knew what might happen? The man might try to carry her off, or otherwise harm her. Worse, he might try to seduce her, or at least win her heart. George himself might have no chance of making an impression on her heart, but that didn't mean he wanted some noble knight to win it instead. George was a man, after all, and as subject to jealousy as anyone else.

George burst out of the trees at a run, and immediately knew something was wrong. Melitta was not by the side of the cellar where he'd left her, which could only mean something had happened to her.

George would never forgive himself.

Twenty-Nine

Time seemed to slow down, for which Melitta was deeply grateful. She ducked out of the way, hearing her tunic tear as the unicorn's horn raked its way through it. Her skin burned, and she knew she been grazed by the beast, too. She ran to the only structure she could see – the well. Putting the stone circle between her and the beast, she dared to turn around to see how close it was. Only to discover that the unicorn still stood beside the tree where she had been standing, only moments earlier.

Melitta crept around the well, in order to get a better view of the beast. Her mouth dropped open in surprise.

In trying to impale her, the unicorn had in fact pinned itself to the tree with its own horn. Try as it might to yank itself free, the beast was stuck. Fearing that it might free itself once again, Melitta ran down the hill for the bag of belongings they'd brought with them. The length of rope they hadn't needed to get George out of the cellar was what she wanted now.

Melitta threw a coil of rope over the beast's neck, securing it with some difficulty as the beast struggled with the tree. Next, she tied the makeshift halter to the tree, looping the rope several times around the trunk before tying it with the strongest knot she knew. There. Let the beast try and break free from that.

Behind her, the horrible unicorn scream sounded again. Melitta whirled, but there was no other beast. Just the one before her. The unicorn tied to the tree let out a frustrated snort. An answering snort came from further down the hill.

They couldn't be two beasts. They couldn't be. And yet…

Melitta checked to make sure the unicorn was securely tied to the tree, then made her way down to the edge of the cellar. To her amazement, there was also a unicorn in the cellar. Looking from one beast to the other, Melitta marvelled. Two unicorns, not one. She would never forget this day.

The beast in the cellar let out another scream, then flopped over on its side, panting. Melitta might not be an expert on horses or unicorns, but she knew this wasn't a good sign. When the beast screamed again, the second one answered it.

For the first time, Melitta dared to slip inside a unicorn's mind. But all she met was a blaze of unbearable pain. Pain in her… arm? No, the pain was not hers. It belonged to the unicorn. He had broken its foreleg when it landed in the cellar, and it could neither walk nor escape.

The second beast had come to its rescue, she assumed. But what use was another unicorn to one trapped in the cellar with a broken leg?

"Melitta? Melitta!" George's shouts became increasingly urgent.

Melitta rose from a crouch and waved. He had the priest with him, she noted. Wonderful. The priest could put the poor animal out of its misery. Or perhaps he knew something about healing horses. She certainly didn't know enough to do anything for the animal.

"How did it get out?" George burst out, catching sight of the second unicorn.

Melitta wanted to sink back down to the ground, she suddenly felt so exhausted. But she didn't want to look weak in front of the priest, who was still the client, after all. "It didn't," she said, pointing. "The first beast is in the cellar. The second beast came to save it, I think." She peered into the cellar again. "Come here. I think it's broken its leg. We have to help it somehow."

"Two unicorns!" the priest breathed, so eager to see inside the cellar that he almost knocked Melitta over the edge.

"Are you going to put it out of its misery, Father?" she asked. "Or miraculously heal its leg?"

The priest's eyes shone, but he didn't seem to see her anymore. "Miracles. Miracles on such a holy site," he muttered. "That's what we must have. A miracle." Like a man possessed, he headed for the well.

"No, Father!" George shouted, running after the priest to hold him back.

But the priest would not be stopped. He drew a pail of water from the well, but he didn't stop to drink it this time. No third unicorn appeared to attack him, either.

With the bucket dangling from one arm, the priest climbed down the ladder Melitta hadn't seen before into the cellar with the injured unicorn.

"He will be killed," George said. "We must

stop him."

Melitta shook her head. "Wait. He said the water can work miracles. The unicorn is the guardian of the well. Surely the well would want to help him."

Down in the cellar, the priest blessed the bucket of water, before pouring it in a thin trickle over the beast's leg. When the bucket was empty, he tossed it up to the grass at Melitta's feet. "Fetch me more water," the priest commanded.

George hurried to obey.

The priest pulled the beast's leg straight, then poured the second bucket over it in the same manner. Five times he sent George back for more water, until the cellar floor was awash, but neither man or beast seem to care. When George brought up the empty bucket, Melitta filled it with grass instead and send him back to the priest with it. "Perhaps he is hungry," she said softly. "When a witch used powerful healing magic on me, I remember I woke absolutely starving."

The priest grabbed a handful of grass, which the unicorn happily lipped from his hand. "Remarkable," he said.

"Are you going to kill him?" Melitta demanded. From where she was standing, there was absolutely no doubt that the priest was tending to a male unicorn.

"Never," the priest replied, reaching out to stroke the unicorn's flank. He looked up at George and Melitta, standing on the edge above him, as if seeing them for the first time. "We must build steps to get him out of the cellar immediately."

"You do what you must," George said firmly. "We only came to catch a unicorn for you, and we caught two. It seems to me we have done our job, and it only remains for you to pay the sum that was promised, and we shall be on our way. Building is best left to those who know how to do it."

"An abbey with a holy well that works miracles, and two unicorn guardians. This will be the holiest place for miles around." The priest nodded. "You shall be richly rewarded."

And that, Melitta reflected, might be the first time a hero was ever paid for not slaughtering the beast he was contracted to kill. And the world would be a better place for it.

<h1 style="text-align:center">Thirty</h1>

Loaded with more coin than George thought fair for capturing what were little more than angry horses, he and Melitta set off that evening in search of an inn where they could spend the night.

Yet as the sun began to sink, the largest settlement they encountered was a cluster of houses with not enough people to support an inn. One of the farmers offered space in his barn, and George was of half a mind to accept, but Melitta shook her head slightly, so he declined the offer. Instead, they bought food supplies for several days' travel and continued on their way.

By nightfall, George was ready to set up camp in the first clearing they saw beside the road. Melitta looked just as tired, so when he saw a likely spot, he called a halt. This time, she didn't argue.

They soon had a fire going, and Melitta demonstrated she was quite the expert at toasting bread and cheese.

"Where did you learn to do that?" George demanded over his third golden-brown morsel.

Melitta laughed. "In the convent, when I was a little girl. Mother loved to weave and sometimes grew quite distracted by whatever project she was working on. One of the older nuns used to toast bread and cheese for me, but she'd died of a summer fever, so I took out a toasting fork and tried to do it myself. I got burned a lot to start with, but then I got better. By the time Mother noticed, I was so good at it, I was allowed to make hers, too." She glanced at the sack of food. "Is there pork? Slices of cold roast pork or a smoked leg of ham crisp up quite nicely over a hot fire."

George dug out a joint of meat he couldn't identify in the firelight, and sliced some off for her. "If it's as good as what you do with cheese, my belly is ready to worship you and your cooking skills forever."

Melitta let out a decidedly unladylike snort. "You should see what Queen Margareta's cooks create for feast days. I can cook well enough not to starve, but they can roast meat so that it fair melts in your mouth. They can make cabbage fit for kings, and their dumplings…I used to eat so many dumplings it's a wonder I wasn't sick. I used to have competitions with the little princesses, to see who could eat the most dumplings. I was bigger, so I always won, but when the little prince joined in, he ate too many and he was sick all night. The queen forbade any more contests after that."

George's blood ran cold. One moment she

was the girl of his dreams, and the next...so far out of reach his dreams were laughable. Melitta was raised with royalty, and she deserved a prince. Not him.

"It sounds so perfect," he said slowly, uncorking a skin of mead that had come with the food. He drank deeply, then passed it to Melitta. "If life in the castle was so good, why did you ever leave?"

She took a swig. "I think it was the princess's betrothal gown. She was to be betrothed to some neighbouring prince, and both of them younger than I am. I looked at the dress, and the court, and I realised that if I didn't do something, this was all my future would hold. Sewing dresses for the queen and her daughters. Watching them marry princes while I..." She sighed. "Mother offered to make a match for me. Any man I wanted at court, she said. Queen Margareta has always regarded me like one of her children, for she and Mother have been friends since I was a baby, so she would have made sure I married a man befitting my station. But when I looked at all the young noblemen, practising their archery or swordplay in the training grounds, I wanted none of them."

Melitta tipped the skin up, gulping down almost as much as George had. "It's the mind-reading, you see. It's a curse as much as it's a blessing. For all the couples who claim to be happily married, I know the truth. I know who is loved and who is not, who is terrible in the bedchamber and who is such a perfect lover anyone would swoon to be with them. I know everyone, inside and out, their secrets and their shames, and no one ever changes. I was trapped in a gilded cage from which I thought I should never get out…until that knight came. And then you, calling for those who wanted to be heroes. And you…you picked me. Out of all those boys who talked of nothing else for days, lining up to be considered for the apprenticeship…you picked me." She drank again, but spilled some of it down her tunic. Swearing, she tried to mop up the mess.

George couldn't tear his eyes away from the patch of skin showing at her belly. "What knight?" he asked, trying and failing to curb his jealousy.

"Sir…I think his name was Sir Chase. Highly skilled at archery. But not so skilled at diplomacy. He offended the queen and she banished him from her court. I never saw him but the once. It was what he said that stuck with me, though. He said a hero was more than a sword. More than his weapons and armour and skill on the battlefield. That his wit and honour were worth more than anything. And that to a true hero, every woman was equal to a queen when it came to who was worth saving."

Melitta tugged her tunic down and for the first time, George saw the dark stains across it. The cloth was torn, too, with the worst stains creeping from the ragged edges.

"Is that blood?" he demanded, reaching for the hem of her tunic.

Melitta glanced down. "Probably. I should

wash. I'd intended to order some hot water so that I might bathe properly once we reached an inn, but – "

"Is that your blood?"

"I imagine so. Neither of the unicorns was injured."

George jumped to his feet and paced around the fire. "We should have stopped at that hamlet, where you could have received aid. We should have used some of that holy water to heal you. If I'd known you were hurt…My lady, please forgive me. Let me see what I can do to help."

"There's no need," Melitta said, yanking up the hem of her tunic so that her belly was bared. "Look, the cuts have closed already. The graze is still a little raw, I'll allow, but by morning it will have healed, too."

George's mouth went dry. He shoved away the inappropriate thoughts that crowded into his head to really look at what she showed him. He traced the line that matched the rip across her tunic. How had she not been eviscerated?

"When did this happen?"

"Today, when the second unicorn charged me. I didn't move fast enough, so her horn scraped a little skin off on her way past." Melitta shrugged. "It hurt at first, but then I forgot about it. The other beast needed healing more than I did." Down went the soft wool, covering her belly.

"Today." George shook his head. It wasn't possible. "Normal people don't heal that fast."

Melitta managed a smile. "Mind-reading isn't normal, either. My gifts were never particularly useful in the castle. Now…I don't mind them so much."

"But…how?"

"When I was younger, I fell ill. So ill my mother thought I would die. The queen found a witch who specialises in healing, and she tried her magic on me. She cast a spell so powerful she fainted for days afterwards, Mother said. When I awoke, I was healed completely. The sickness was gone, and it has not returned. It wasn't until a few weeks later, when I tripped on the stairs and barked my shin, that I realised what else had changed. Within hours, my skin had healed itself, so even I could barely see the damage the next morning. I have never known a day of illness since, and all the times I pricked my fingers while sewing became little more than a momentary nuisance."

George laughed bitterly. "I wish my fairy godmother had given me gifts like yours. Instead, I think too much, so I am slow to act. But she gifted me with fleet feet, so that when I am in danger, they will take me far and fast to save me, like a coward. She gave me an enchanted sword, too, but I lost that the same day. To a dragon."

Melitta headed for her saddlebags and rifled through them until she found a fresh tunic. She turned her back on George and tugged off the torn one. He stared at the fine curves of her shoulders, her back, her hips as they framed her bottom, wishing, longing for what he couldn't have, before she smoothed a fresh tunic over all that temptation.

She flung her cloak around her shoulders and returned to the fire. She sat beside George, reaching over to pat his knee. "You're not a coward, you know. You stood at my side and shot those giants, showing no fear. Why, you even chased one down. If you hadn't run from the boar or the unicorn, both of them might have killed you. You're the bravest hero I've ever met, for you faced all of those things with a maiden at your side. I'm no hero, I know that, though I try. I couldn't kill the unicorn yesterday and when that giant tackled me to the ground, he would have killed me for certain, if you hadn't shot him first. You may not be a knight, but you have the wits and honour to be one, if you wished it." Her eyes seemed to burn into his as they reflected the flames. "Return with me to Queen Margareta's court at Aros. Once I tell her all the things you have done, she will knight you, I am sure of it."

Her hand was warm on his, but George

knew he could never accept what she offered. "I cannot. I ran from a dragon once, and my cowardice still haunts me. I will not rest until the dragon is dead, or I am."

Instead of turning away from him in disgust, Melitta's lovely eyes widened. "What happened?"

Swallowing back his shame, George told her. Every painful detail, from the first folly of wanting to face the dragon in the field to his final, ignominious defeat.

And when his voice died away, he found her head resting on his shoulder, for she was fast asleep.

Laughing quietly to himself, George gently laid her on the ground and wrapped her cloak around her. He supposed his story was boring to a girl who was the earthly embodiment of the goddess of war. He banked the fire and dug out his own cloak so that he might get some sleep, too.

Thirty-One

Melitta woke up warmer than she expected. When she opened her eyes, she realised why. Somehow during the night, she'd cuddled up to George, and she could feel the heat of him even through the thickness of her cloak.

She edged away from him, wishing that they had managed to find an inn to spend the night in. She almost wished they'd accepted the offer of that barn, but she wouldn't go that far.

That particular hamlet had been poor enough before the giants turned up, and when travel slowed along that particular road, the giants hadn't been averse to stealing from them. Now, with their best breeding stock long gone into the giants' bellies, and their women sent who knew where, some of those men had been desperate enough to consider robbing travellers for their own profit. Not wanting to be their first victim, Melitta had asked to buy supplies from the farmers. If she'd paid twice what the food was worth, no one had commented on it. She hoped that the return of travellers along their road, now the giants were gone, might help them more than turning bandit themselves.

Or it might do nothing. Melitta would never know, as she wasn't likely to travel this road again.

She sighed as she crouched down to stir up the fire, searching for a hot coal among the ashes. She soon had it burning merrily again, with flames hot enough to toast some of yesterday's bread. Even with the fire going, the brisk morning wasn't warm enough for her to want to take off her cloak. Not for the first time, she wished she hadn't cut off her hair as the breeze sent icy fingers tickling her neck. Melitta pulled up her hood.

"Are you cold, my lady?" George crouched down beside her and set another piece of wood on the fire. "From behind, you looked like a witch casting some sort of spell."

Melitta laughed. "There are those who say that my mind-reading gift makes me a sort of witch, if not the spellcasting kind. But seeing as you called my cooking magical last night, perhaps I am casting a spell over breakfast after all." She offered him the stick she'd used to skewer her toast.

Melitta rose and busied herself saddling her horse and fastening her saddlebags. She'd remembered George's story about the dragon last night, and, more importantly, she'd remembered her unanswered questions.

"You never did tell me. Where is the dragon we're supposed to face, and when will we do it?" she asked.

George dropped his food in the fire. "What?"

"You told me last night how you fought the dragon, and failed. I saw in your mind that you believe we can win, together. So when are we doing this? Or am I still not ready?" Much though she hated to admit it, Melitta didn't feel any more like a hero than when she'd first set out. Without her bow, her archery hadn't improved. Her sword skills were still rudimentary at best and she might have killed a few men, and the boar, before she helped trap two unicorns, but none of that felt particularly heroic.

Whereas a dragon…that was the sort of monster only a hero could conquer.

George uncorked the water skin and took a drink. "My lady, you were ready the very day I met you, and no mistake. If anyone can defeat a dragon, it is you. After all I've seen you do already, I have no doubt of that. It is me who may not be ready, and to tell the truth, I may never be. What if I run away again?"

Did he really believe that? Melitta's heart swelled in her chest. With pride, no less.

"I couldn't have done any of what I have without you. All of the monsters we've vanquished, we've done it together," she said warmly. "And with the assistance of your fleet feet, as you call them. A hero is more than his sword or armour. It takes cunning and honour and so much more to do what we have done. We shall find this dragon, face it, and we shall defeat it. And we'll do it without enchanted swords and other such silly things. We'll have what other knights won't. We'll have a plan."

For a moment, George raised his eyes to her, and they were filled with hope. "I want to believe you, but what if I run? I will never forgive myself if I leave you to face the beast alone."

Melitta smiled. "Last night, you told me of all the men who had faced the dragon before you. How they stood and fought, until they died. Whatever we do, and however we do this, there must be a way to put those fleet feet of yours to good use. They helped you outrun a dragon once. I bet you could do it again. We'll need a bigger cellar, though."

"Have you ever seen a dragon? They have wings. They can fly."

Melitta swallowed. "No, I've never seen one. But you have. Which is why I need your help. What do you say, George? Time to go kill a dragon?"

George bowed low. "Whatever my lady wishes."

Thirty-Two

Kasmirus had changed little since George left, he found, as they entered the gates. But the people of Kasmirus…they had altered considerably, and not for the better. An air of melancholy surrounded the town like some deadly miasma. Though it was Sunday, everyone wore dark, funereal colours.

George's blood ran cold. He stopped the first man he recognised, a baker he'd often bought bread from. "Please, tell me. What ails the city? Is it plague?" For nothing else could send a whole city into mourning, surely.

The baker shook off George's grasp. "By all that's holy, I hope not. Is a dragon not enough for our sins? When I think of those poor girls…I won't let my daughters leave the house now, for it is not safe. The sooner some knight dispatches the dragon, the happier we'll all be."

He got no more information from the next two people he asked, so George headed for an inn frequented by wealthy merchant visitors to the city. A more costly establishment than he might have chosen for himself, but he had a bag full of the abbey's coin and Melitta's comfort to think of.

Sure enough, when he showed he had the coin to pay for the room, the landlord lost interest in him, directing a chambermaid to take them to their rooms.

Melitta ordered hot water to be sent up so that she might wash, and George left her to her ablutions, promising to spend the time listening to gossip in the taproom downstairs.

The common room was nearly empty, and

the merchants George met knew little of the goings-on in the city, being but recently arrived themselves. Finally, in desperation, he asked the barman what he knew about the dragon.

"Only that the king has promised half the kingdom and a lordship to the man who slays the beast," the barman replied. "Many have tried, but none have succeeded." He squinted at George. "Are you thinking of trying your luck?"

"Perhaps," George replied defensively.

The barman laughed. "Take my advice, Sir Knight. Climb back on your horse and ride far away from here. That dragon brings death to anyone who goes near it, and none can withstand it. The only reason I stay in the city is that it is too dangerous to travel. The beast preys on travellers now, too, as his appetite grows. Soon, we may not have any trade at all, if the dragon develops a taste for merchants, too."

Talk turned to the current high prices of trade goods, which the merchants toasted with another round of wine, so George thanked the barman and headed back upstairs to share what he'd learned with Melitta.

A lordship and half the kingdom. That wouldn't turn him into a prince, but perhaps it would be enough for Melitta to consider allowing him to court her.

He fought down a laugh. All he had to do was defeat a dragon, and survive. Then he could beg the goddess of war for her hand.

He knocked on Melitta's door, but received no answer. He knocked a second time, before calling her name.

The door creaked ajar, revealing a red-eyed Melitta. A tear rolled down her cheek, and she wiped it away. "The vile beast must die," she said through gritted teeth.

George grinned. "On that, we agree."

Thirty-Three

Melitta could feel George's curiosity at her tears, but she couldn't seem to stop the flow. She'd opened her mind to the townspeople while she lay in the bath, and though she'd closed herself off from their thoughts since, their vast grief still roiled within her.

Those girls. Those poor girls…

"That vile beast must die."

George agreed wholeheartedly. How had she ever thought him a coward?

Haltingly, she began her tale. The tale of a

city in mourning.

The words came slowly, describing the images lifted from so many minds, but the gist was the same.

On the day the priests blessed the fleet in the name of Our Lady, they had led a great procession out of the city toward the river. In the forefront of the throng was a statue of the Blessed Virgin, carried by four virgin princesses dressed in white wool to match the robes on the statue.

The dragon had flown overhead, as it did so often that they took little notice of it. It flew across the countryside, stealing and devouring sheep in the fields, before retreating into its cave, only coming out when it hungered or some hero challenged it.

That day had been different. Perhaps because they wore white wool, or perhaps the dragon was simply curious. He shot a gout of flame before him, enveloping the girls and the statue in searing heat. While the girls screamed, the beast had devoured them, and the statue, too.

The people of the city had watched in horror before fleeing back inside the walls to hide from the dragon.

On the morrow, the king had offered to reward the dragonslayer with half his kingdom, but no one had claimed the reward.

Even now, Melitta could feel the beast stomping about in the caverns beneath the city where it lived. Waiting. Watching. For who would be next?

It was one thing for the beast to kill knights who challenged it, but another to kill and devour innocents. Those girls hadn't deserved to die.

Melitta made up her mind. "That dragon wouldn't understand honour if it climbed up its bottom. We're going to play dirty."

George looked intrigued. "How?"

"What do you know about killing dragons?"

He shrugged. "I know my namesake killed one with a sword, using a maiden for bait. I've always wondered about that."

Melitta's anger rose, not at George, but at his saintly namesake. "So it seems even saints have no honour when it comes to killing dragons. Fine. But no maidens. We'll use a sheep."

"A sheep."

Melitta took a deep breath and told George what she planned to do.

Thirty-Four

Feeling terribly exposed, George rolled the barrel to the mouth of the dragon's cave. He draped the sheepskin over it and prayed that it would be enough to fool the beast. Once the bait was in place, George took to his heels and fled. Not to the city, but to a high vantage point where Melitta waited.

Together, they crouched amid the leaves of an oak Melitta had chosen for its good view of the cave mouth.

They didn't have to wait long. The dragon

had heard George, and it emerged from the darkness, sniffing the air.

George gulped. If the beast could smell him, it would find them.

The beast lowered its snout and sniffed delicately at the woolly barrel. Then it opened its mouth, enveloping the barrel in searing flame.

"Oh, no," Melitta murmured.

While the barrel still burned, the dragon wrapped its tongue around it and tugged the whole thing into its mouth. Tipping its head back, the beast swallowed it whole.

"Yes!"

George didn't dare make a sound.

"Do you think we put enough arsenic in the barrel to kill a dragon?" she asked.

George shrugged. "We filled it to the brim. That much poison could kill an army. Surely it's enough for a dragon."

He didn't voice his biggest worry – how would they know if it was dead? If it was deep in the caves, he didn't want to go in after it only to discover the beast was alive and well.

Melitta tapped her head. "I can feel it. Dragons are magical beasts and their minds are…different. I don't even need to concentrate to hear its thoughts. I wish I could block it out. It's a vile creature. Like some humans, it enjoys killing."

Now the true wait began. George did his best not to doze off, but it was hard. Melitta stayed alert, and she'd wake him when she could no longer sense the beast, surely.

"It's coming out. The poison is working," she said eventually, excitement burning in her eyes.

A long moment later, George glimpsed movement inside the cave. The dragon staggered out, looking for all the world as if it had drunk too much ale.

George held his breath. He could almost taste victory, it was so close.

The dragon slumped to the ground, opening its mouth as if gasping for air.

Fighting for its last breath. Good, George

thought.

Then it vomited up a steaming mess. Once. Twice.

The dragon shook its head, coughed, then ambled back inside its cave.

"It's feeling better," Melitta whispered, sounding disappointed.

George wanted to rage at the heavens. The dragon deserved to die in agony, not survive an attempt to poison it.

"Perhaps it's immune to poison. We'll have to try something else," she said.

Thirty-Five

In the common room of the inn that night, Melitta threw her hands up in despair. "I don't know any more. I've never had to kill clever vermin before."

"Beg pardon, mistress." An elderly merchant rose from his seat and bowed in her direction. "Did I hear you say you need to kill rats that are too clever?"

Melitta opened her mouth to tell the man to mind his own business.

"Because one of my warehouses had a

terrible problem with rats, but my steward told me an old wives' tale he swore worked. See, poisoning works for a while, but then they grow wise to that, seeing their friends die when they eat poisoned food, until none will touch it. You may try a new poison, but they'll learn about that, too. My steward swore he knew a poison that they'd never suspect. He painted all the walls and containers with a white powder he called lime. Now, the stuff's not poisonous on its own. Oh, no. But it makes a body powerfully thirsty, because it's salty, see. So the beasts eat it and think they're safe. Then they go for water, drinking as much as they can hold. And that's what kills 'em, because the water works some magic on the lime and they explode. Poof!" He demonstrated with his hands.

Exploding rats. What would he come up with next? Melitta forced down the retort she wanted to make and tried to think of a way to thank him so that he'd go away.

"You know, that could work," George said,

nodding. He raised his tankard. "My thanks, sir." He signalled for the barman to get the man another drink.

"You're welcome." The man returned to his seat.

Melitta eyed George. "Are you serious? Or have you drunk too much wine?"

"He's right about lime. If you put throw a piece in a bucket of water, it bubbles and steams like it's boiling. If you put enough of that inside a dragon with a lot of water and whatever makes it breathe fire, you'd scald it from the inside out."

"Would a barrel be enough?"

George drained his tankard and smiled. "On the morrow, we shall see."

Thirty-Six

George rolled the barrel of lime to the mouth of the cave. This time, they'd smothered the sheepskin in mutton fat to disguise the smell. He prayed it would work as he jogged back to Melitta's treetop perch.

Once again, the dragon emerged and devoured the barrel disguised as a sheep before heading back into its cave.

They didn't have to wait long before the beast ambled out again, and headed for the river. George watched in satisfaction as it drank and drank. Surely when the water mixed with the lime, it would be enough.

The dragon turned and made its way back toward its lair, more slowly this time as if the mixture in its belly was affecting it.

Now George tasted victory. True victory.

"Hey, dragon!" a voice roared. "Come and fight me!"

A knight appeared, swaggering toward the beast with his sword held high.

The dragon peered at the armoured man, then staggered toward him.

"That idiot's going to steal our kill!" George protested, climbing down as fast as he could go. "Hey! You! That dragon's ours!" he shouted as he sprinted toward the beast.

Not fast enough. The dragon lowered its head and unleashed a gout of flame.

The armoured man screamed as flames enveloped him. Then the sound died, and the smell of burning flesh reached George.

The dragon turned its head, fixing one slitted eye on him. For a moment, George could have sworn recognition flared in that look. But it couldn't be. Dragons weren't that bright.

Then a thick, muscled tail came out of nowhere and knocked him flat. Again.

And the world went dark. Again.

Thirty-Seven

Melitta reached the ground a moment behind George, but she was no match for him when it came to sheer speed. She suspected no man could beat him, so powerful was his godmother's gift.

She wanted to shout after him, to warn him that the dragon wasn't weakened, that they couldn't have given it enough lime. But she could scarcely catch her breath as she ran.

The armoured knight became a human torch, and there was nothing she could do to stop it. Tears of frustration sprang to her eyes, but she didn't slow. The dragon had seen George, and it knew him. And remembered.

George was too busy looking at its head that he never saw the tail swing up, sending him flying. Then it lowered its head, drawing flame from deep in its belly to burn him to death, too.

"No you don't, you vile beast!" she screeched. Charred, armoured corpses littered the ground, along with their weapons. Melitta picked up a short sword that looked about her size, though its blade was burned black. "Over here! Let's see if you can get this maiden!" She flapped her woollen tunic.

With agonising slowness, the beast turned its head to regard her.

Curiosity washed over her, but nothing more. The dragon didn't see her as a threat.

Melitta reached down and picked up half a scorched steel breastplate that she slipped over her head. It was far too big, but that didn't matter. She clanged the sword against her armour. "I said over here!"

The dragon burped, releasing a fireball that scorched the ground for a dozen yards. Mercifully, it missed George.

"HERE!" she screamed. She broke into a clumsy run, clanking with every step as she charged at the dragon.

It lowered its head, breathing in deeply, before belching flame.

Her mind locked on the beast's, she read his intention in time, and darted out of its path.

The dragon bellowed, moving its ponderous bulk until it faced her again. Down went the head and Melitta felt the inrush of air as though it reached her own lungs.

Full to bursting. Couldn't...breathe...

It tried to flame, but nothing came out.

Again, it inhaled. And deep inside, something ruptured.

This time, it was the dragon that screamed.

Then all hell broke loose.

Thirty-Eight

George raised his head slightly, wondering why he wasn't dead like the charred, armoured corpse beside him. He felt strange, like this had all happened before.

He heard a scream, a sound so primal it couldn't have come from a human throat. And then the whole world was aflame.

He threw himself flat to the ground to allow the blast to pass over him, praying that he'd survive it, as he must have before. Then the heat passed, and he allowed himself to look.

Flames roared up into the sky from what looked like the carcass of a dragon, and out of the flame came a woman. No, a goddess, whose eyes burned like she'd harnessed hell itself.

"Melitta?" George croaked.

She smiled. "Oh, good, you're not dead." She stabbed a finger behind her. "That bastard is, though. And good riddance."

They'd killed the dragon. Well, she had, really, but had he ever doubted it?

Melitta tugged off her breastplate and let it clang to the ground. "We did it." Her smile was more radiant than the fireball behind her.

George laughed. "We did. You're a hero, my lady." He clambered to his feet and brushed himself off.

"So are you," she said. Then she threw her arms around his neck and kissed him.

George's world blazed white. This time he didn't want to wake up.

Thirty-Nine

With her lips pressed against George's mouth and his arms holding her like the most precious thing in the world, Melitta surrendered to the moment. There was nothing more she wanted than to be here, now, with him. The warmth of a fire at her back and the warmth of his love before her…

Melitta broke away from his kiss, gasping.

"Marry me," he said.

She blinked. Surely she hadn't heard correctly.

"I love you. Marry me, Lady Melitta. I could never love another woman the way I love you."

Perhaps she had.

Then his lips claimed hers again, and nothing else mattered. This was as mind-blowing as every kiss she had ever felt through someone else's thoughts, and yet it was so much more. Because she could feel it, burning within her. Hers. No one else's.

"We're perfect for each other," she said breathlessly. She flapped a hand at the bonfire behind her. "Together, we can do anything."

He laughed and scooped her up in his arms, spinning her around in a circle before heading toward the city.

Any other day, Melitta might have scolded him and told him to put her down. But today…all she wanted was to feel his arms around her.

"The sooner we get back to our lodgings, the better, my lady," he said softly in her ear.

Lodgings. Yes. Where there was a bed.

A cheer rose up as they entered the city gates.

"What's your name, sir?" a page in the king's livery asked.

"George."

"George, you are invited to a feast with the king, where he will grant you the reward you deserve for slaying the dragon," the page said, breathless with excitement.

George's arms tightened around Melitta. "Tomorrow, I will meet with the king. After I have been to my lodgings and changed into clothes more appropriate for the king's court."

But not before Melitta got him out of his clothes and kept him that way for some time, she thought dreamily.

Cheers and congratulations followed them all the way to the inn, until the door shut behind them. Still George didn't set Melitta down until he'd climbed the stairs and reached the door to her room.

She wound her arms around his neck and kissed him deeply. "I want a reward, too," she said, trying to tug him into her chamber.

"Tomorrow," George said.

"No, tonight," Melitta said. "I want you tonight."

George cupped her face in his hands. "My lady, your honour is as dear to me as my own. And I will not share your bed before the king grants us our rightful lands and titles. Only then will we have our true reward." He kissed her lips softly, a whisper of the passion they both felt. "Sleep well, my lady, and I will see you on the morrow."

She stared after him as he headed for his own chamber and closed the door.

Her lips still tingled from his kiss.

Today had been the best day of her life. She sighed in blissful anticipation. And tomorrow would be better still.

Forty

As they broke their fast the following morning, another messenger arrived in the king's livery.

He bowed low to George and said, "His most illustrious majesty King Boleslas invites you to the castle for a feast to celebrate your victory over the dragon. There, before all his court, he will give you all the honours he has promised. You will be named a lord of half the kingdom."

"We will be there," George replied.

The messenger glanced at Melitta. He

seemed lost for words for a moment, then added smoothly, "Of course, a seat will be found at one of the lower tables for your squire. I will see to it." The man hurried off.

Melitta burst out laughing. "I know the light is dim in here…but did he really think I was a boy?"

George smiled fondly. "How many maidens kill dragons? I'm sure in the light of day, he could not fail to recognise your beauty." He frowned. "But you should be at my side, not at one of the lower tables. You earned this as much as I have, if not more."

"I've spent a lifetime sitting at the high table, beside the queen. While a knight may wear what he will, a lady does not sit there without a fine gown. If I sat beside you like this, I would shame you," she told him. What she didn't tell him was that she'd tasted the thoughts of everyone in town last night, and they all believed he was the hero who had slayed their dragon, and that he had somehow saved her from the beast. Changing their minds and enlightening them with the truth would be harder than slaying the beast in the first place. A task Melitta would never be equal to, she feared. Let George receive the rewards and adulation. She would share them with him soon enough. "I am content. I will attend the feast as your squire. No fine gown required. And afterward, we will keep our promises to one another."

George rose. "My first feast at court. My father would not believe it." He took a seat beside the fire. "It's a good thing I have you here to tell me how to behave, or I fear I would make some grave mistake."

"I am sure you won't," Melitta said, sinking down by the fire. "I remember my first feast. I must have been five or six. Mother and Queen…no, she was just Lady Margareta then, had gone without me, and left me in the care of two of the sisters from the priory. I screamed that I wanted to go, and because the sisters were to attend the Harvest Feast, they brought me along to the shuttered balcony where they could share the celebration apart from the revellers.

"I could scarcely sit still. All I wanted was to peer through the shutters at everyone. There was the Harvest Queen, dressed all in gold, though she was a farm girl who only got to be queen for one night. I thought she was the most beautiful woman I'd ever seen, and I wanted to be her, though my mother said I was too high-born for that.

"Then Lady Margareta stood up with King Erik, who was only a prince then, but no less handsome, and joined the dance. Then I forgot the Harvest Queen and dinner and everything…all I wanted was to be a beautiful dancing lady with a prince of her own. I was a lady, the same as she, or so I thought, and that was what my future held.

"I dreamed of dancing and princes and romance for many nights after that. Oh, the dreams of a little girl. Like something out of a fairytale. Where all princes are heroic and handsome and terribly in love with the lady of their dreams."

Melitta peered into her empty cup, then tossed the dregs into the fire, where they hissed and spat.

"It wasn't until a much later feast, where I was wearing as much silk as my mother, that I realised maybe I didn't want a prince, or a husband at all."

George drank drained his cup without looking at her. "So it's not true what you told me in the forest? The real reason why you ran away from home? Because your father was going to force you to marry a prince?"

Melitta laughed so hard she nearly choked. "No, my father is dead. A saint, or so they tell me. And my mother will never force me into a marriage I do not want. She did want me to pick a husband, though."

"But you did run away."

Melitta frowned. "You make it sound like I sneaked away in the dead of night, instead of in the morning light with my mother there to say farewell. I left the life I had because it dawned on me that I wanted to be my own hero, instead of waiting for some knight to save me and fall at my feet. And tonight, I will feel like it is my first feast all over again. You will sit at the high table, and I will watch in anonymity from the lower tables. But this time, I won't envy the ladies sitting up there with you."

He bowed his head. "Very well, my lady. I find it difficult to believe that someone like you who was promised a prince could possibly choose a lowly shoemaker like me. If I were you, I would take the promised prince, for who can refuse royalty?"

Melitta just smiled. There was no point telling him that when you could see in the minds of everyone, there was very little difference between a prince and a peasant. All men had hopes and dreams and desires, and she wanted the man who shared hers, no matter what his title.

And tonight they would share…everything.

Forty-One

When George took his seat at the high table, he had to admit it was a heady experience. Never had he seen so many people crowded into one room before, and all of them so richly dressed. He glanced down at his own simple clothes, but Melitta had assured him they were good enough. The court wanted to see a fighter, a hero, the man who had slayed their dragon scourge. Still, it didn't help him to not feel self-conscious when everyone around him wore silks at bright as flowers while he wore wool.

Fine wool, for he could afford it, but wool nonetheless. And right now, it made him itch like the coarsest stuff imaginable with all those eyes on him. How did Melitta stand such scrutiny?

Only now did he understand why she didn't want to sit at the high table. So many people staring…

Then the food was served, and it wasn't so bad.

The king had seated him on the end, beside a girl in blue who said nothing and refused to look at him. How he would have preferred to have Melitta by his side. And when they were married, he would. Not even the king would refuse to give his lady all the honours that were accorded to him.

George scanned the crowded tables, looking for the only woman he wanted. Past the courtiers, knights and their ladies, the colours grew duller as the benches were filled with men-at-arms — no women there. Except

Melitta. She perched on the end of a bench near the window, nibbling at something on the point of her dagger. The men at the table – no, boys, all of them, he realised. Squires to the knights, most likely. The boys ignored her, talking among themselves and paying her no attention at all.

George raged at them. Didn't they realise they had a hero in their midst? A lady, no less, who had slayed a dragon?

Evidently not, for they all laughed at something one of the boys had said, while she sat there calmly.

The food was plentiful and the wine flowed freely, though George partook sparingly of both. He didn't want to make a fool of himself when the king called him up to receive his reward. What if he stumbled and fell? Or said something that offended the king?

By all that was holy, he needed Melitta by his side, helping him. He was nothing without her. And yet, she sat at the other end of the hall, oblivious to his eyes on her.

What if she'd changed her mind?

George fretted through the interminable feast, heartily wishing he never had to attend another. Maybe this was what Melitta meant about not missing such things. How much food and wine could a man consume? Surely they were all sated by now, he thought, but servants kept bringing out more platters and jugs.

Finally, King Boreslas rose to his unsteady feet. He'd had more to drink than most, George judged, watching him sway.

"My subjects!" the king cried. "Lord, ladies, knights, men! We are here to celebrate a great victory. Sir George has defeated the dragon that oppressed us for so long." He raised his cup in a toast. The whole hall cheered, and drank with him as he emptied his cup. "And he shall be rewarded!"

More cheers, even louder still.

"Kneel, Sir George!"

This was the part Melitta had explained to him in painstaking detail. He hoped he didn't forget anything.

George dropped to one knee before the king, then pulled his sword out of its scabbard. He laid the blade across his open palms and held the weapon out.

"I pledge my honour and obedience to you, Your Majesty. My life to your service, as God is my witness." George prayed he'd remembered the words right. Melitta had said it didn't matter if he made a mistake — no two men seemed to state their vow of service in the same way.

King Boreslas inclined his head and took the proffered sword. Wrapping both hands around the hilt, he muttered some words in Latin that George didn't understand. He finished with, "Rise, Lord George, and take up your blade in my service." He presented George's sword, hilt-first, back to him.

George slid the blade back into its scabbard, as Melitta had advised him. With his back to the hall, he couldn't see if she was smiling or shaking her head in mortification.

The hall erupted in more cheering, so he hoped he hadn't made too great a fool of himself.

"And as a final reward for his heroism, I have decided to bestow my only remaining daughter, Princess Sativa, on him in marriage, this very night. My personal confessor and priest will marry them in the castle chapel after the feast, and if I'm not mistaken, Lord George will have an heir on the way before the night is through!"

Laughter and cheering echoed through the hall as men toasted George's marriage and virility. Even the priest rose to his feet and he nearly fell over, he was so drunk.

King Boreslas ushered the girl in blue forward to kneel beside George. He spouted more Latin, then announced that he had blessed their union.

George's mouth was dry, and not in a good way.

He couldn't marry the princess. Couldn't accept her as a bride. It was Melitta he wanted, no one else. The princess beside him continued to ignore him, just as she had for the rest of the feast. He couldn't marry a girl who pretended he didn't exist, no matter how grateful her father was.

"And when God sees fit to end my reign, Lord George will ascend the throne in my place!"

George could have sworn his heart dropped right into his boots. Heir to a throne? No. Not him. This was preposterous. He was barely even a hero. He couldn't be a king.

"As my heir, you must sit at my right hand, Lord George!"

People shuffled along the benches at the high table to make space for George, who staggered to take his place beside the king.

"Now, who will be the first to declare their oath of loyalty to Lord George?" King Boreslas declared, his gaze sweeping the hall.

Courtiers rushed from their seats to be the first, crowding before the high table so that George couldn't see past them.

Melitta. What would she think of this? Being a lord was one thing, but one day a king…she didn't like court. She would never consent to be a queen. And then there was the matter of the princess he didn't want. But how could he tell a king that his daughter wasn't good enough to be his bride? George would be lucky to keep his head.

Melitta would know what to do. Melitta would help him deal with this mess. Unless she believed he had thrown her aside to marry the princess…

He rose onto his toes, straining to look past the crowd so that he might see her, catch her eye and beg for her help. But she was nowhere in sight.

George's world crumbled around him. Without her, he had nothing.

Forty-Two

As benches scraped and men rose to pay their respects to their new overlord, Melitta made her way to the back of the hall. She knew good manners decreed that she should congratulate George on his good fortune, and on his bride, but she wasn't sure that anything she said would be considered good manners tonight.

She climbed the stairs to her chamber, where she packed up the little she had, and decided to leave George a note. It would be hours before the dragonslaying lord would find it, by which time she would be well away, she was certain. What need did he have for her anyway? He had his bride, his lands, his lordship – everything he had ever wanted. Melitta fought down a sob. He didn't need and definitely didn't want her. After all, who'd choose a mere lady when he could have a princess? He'd said as much this morning. Even last night, he'd hinted that it wouldn't have been honourable to give in to their desires. She'd thought he meant delaying by a day, but evidently she'd misunderstood. Instead, he'd meant that today he would marry a princess, and she would have what? Permission to watch? Melitta wanted to give him a piece of her mind about that, too.

Yet when she faced the empty piece of parchment with a quill in hand, she still did not know what to say. She had to write something, she knew. Dipping her quill in the ink, Melitta forced herself to write what was right.

I congratulate you, Lord George, she wrote. My best wishes for your future health and happiness. Should you ever have need to hire a slayer of monsters, you will find me…

Here she stopped. For where would he find her? Her first thought was to return home, as she had promised her mother, but Melitta wasn't sure she could go back to her old life. She liked the adventure of the life she had led since she left home. She would not easily give up her leathers for silks once more.

Finally, she wrote: You will find me where I am needed most.

Vague but probably the best she could come up with at the time, she decided.

She sealed the scroll with a blob of wax and left it on the table in her room. It was all she left behind, for little remained of her childish dreams of love, marriage, and happiness.

Shouldering her saddlebags, Melitta headed down to the stables. She would saddle her horse and be gone before anyone thought to ask for her. By the time George read her message and thought to look for her, she would be safely asleep in an inn in the next town. Perhaps, if she was lucky, she would have already found information about her next quest. Unbidden, a smile sprang to her lips at the thought. The people of Kasimus might not believe a maiden could slay monsters, but she would show them. She was a dragonslayer now.

The stables were surprisingly quiet, for all that they were full of horses. Oh, the horses made plenty of noise, but there was no one about. Even the stable hands were off celebrating this night. After all, it wasn't every day someone slayed a dragon that had plagued your city. The whole city was celebrating.

Yet Melitta heard the clink of harness and was instantly on the alert. "Who's there?" she demanded, sliding her dagger from its sheath. "Show yourself!"

The clinking ceased, but no one appeared. Melitta was not fooled. Carefully, she bit her lip and sent her thoughts out, questing for the mind of what she suspected was a horse thief.

But the jumbled mind she touched was no

thief at all.

I will not be a prize, the distinctly feminine thoughts repeated to herself. I will not be handed over as a prize. I am a princess, not some bauble!

Melitta's horse thief could be none other than the Princess Sativa, George's intended bride. An unwilling bride, Melitta realised uneasily.

Forgetting her own hurry to leave, Melitta made her way to the stall where the princess hid behind a horse. "Princess?" Melitta ventured. "Why are you not at the feast, celebrating with everyone else?"

Melitta had to give the girl credit. The princess stepped out of hiding, her chin held high. "You shall not stop me," the girl insisted. "I am not a prize to be won. I will not be handed to that shoemaker in marriage like some pretty bauble."

Melitta balked at the girl's tone. "George is no mere shoemaker," she said, frowning. "True, he was once a master shoemaker. But he is also a hero, a slayer of monsters and giants. He has saved maidens and whole towns from monsters. And he slayed a dragon at the very gates to your city. Your father has seen fit to make him a lord and give him lands to match. Any girl would be lucky to be allowed to marry such a man." Melitta had to swallow hard against the lump in her throat as she said this. She would consider herself lucky to marry George, lordship and lands notwithstanding. This spoiled princess, royalty though she might be, did not deserve him.

"I will not be a prize," the princess repeated stubbornly.

Only then did Melitta realise that the clinking harness she had heard was the saddle and bridle the horse behind the princess now wore. The princess would rather flee than marry George.

"He does not love me," the princess continued. "Though I sat beside him, he scarcely even looked at me. He had eyes for only one person in the feasting hall." She glared at Melitta. "You. The one he calls his squire, but you are more than that, aren't you? You are his lover."

Melitta tried hard not to laugh. She loved him, she knew that. But she had never shared his bed, not in the way the princess meant, and now she never would. For he was to marry this girl and Melitta was nothing to him. "I am not his lover. I am his partner, in that we slayed the dragon together. We have slayed many beasts together, but I think his hero days are done."

"Lover or not, his heart belongs to you," the princess said bitterly. "You shall not stop me. I ride to the coast, and my betrothed. A man who loves me, or at least he did once."

Melitta's heart ached for the girl, for she saw herself in this proud princess. Both fled their homes in search of a better life they imagined lay outside the castle, though they sought very different things. Which was a sillier goal, though — love, or a dragon? Melitta couldn't suppress a smile. A dragon, of course, for she knew love existed.

So did Princess Sativa.

"Take only what you need with you," Melitta urged. "Food, water, weapons, and clothes that are suited for rough travel. Nothing that will mark you for what you are, because there are men on the roads who will take advantage of a lady. They will see you as even more of a prize." Melitta was tempted to tell the girl exactly what sort of prize those brigands had thought her, but she wasn't sure even that would make the princess change her mind. After all, Melitta had known, but she'd gone anyway. "You would be safer in your father's castle."

The princess drew herself up. "What would you know of it? A girl pretending to be a squire knows nothing of the cage that is a royal court."

Melitta laughed. "Forgive me, your royal highness, but I was raised in a royal court, a princess in all but name, alongside Queen Margareta's own children. And I could take my place at her side again tomorrow, if I wished. But I will not leave these walls without my armour, my weapons, and enough money and provisions for the journey, because I know there are monsters out there." She pulled a dagger from its ankle sheath and held it out to Princess Sativa. "Take it, princess, for I promise you will have need of it."

Sativa swept aside her cape, revealing two sheathed daggers strapped to her girdle. "I am not a fool."

Melitta sincerely hoped the girl was right. Still, she dug through her bag until she found a clean tunic and hose. "Then at least take these. Court dresses will be no use to you on your journey."

Sativa hesitated, then took the clothing. "I thank you. But I must repay you, and I will need all the coin I have for my journey, as you say. Wait." She disappeared back into the horse stall.

Melitta fought not to tap her foot in impatience.

Finally, the princess emerged, wearing Melitta's spare clothes. "They are finer than they look. Here, consider this a gift." She thrust a wad of silk at Melitta.

"I have no need for silk," Melitta replied, realising too late that she held the princess's feast gown. "Oh, no. I cannot wear this."

"Every priest in the city is so drunk they cannot tell the difference between one woman and another. Yet in an hour, my father will command one of them to conduct a wedding, marrying me to the shoemaker. If you wear this, they will think you are me. Marry the man, if that is your wish. By morning, it will be too late for anyone to do anything. I will be gone and you will be his wife." Sativa's eyes implored her. "Please."

"My lady? Are you here, or am I too late?" a male voice called. George.

The princess paled. "He cannot catch me here. He will stop me!"

A princess too proud to beg for help. Melitta made no attempt to hide her smile.

Rescuing maidens in distress was what heroes did, and she was every bit as much a hero as George.

Who had eyes for only one woman at the feast, hmm? Perhaps Melitta might stay after all, and marry such a man. And in so doing, save a princess.

Lifting her chin, Melitta marched out of the stables. "Lord George," she greeted him.

George sagged in relief. "Thank God. I thought you'd left. Melitta, I swear I didn't know about the princess. I must speak to the king, tell him I cannot…"

Melitta silenced him with a wave of her hand. "Ah, but you can. I have it on good authority that the princess will not attend your wedding. But I have a mind to. Give me a moment, for I must be properly dressed."

They found an empty chamber, and George guarded the door while Melitta changed into the princess's gown. The silk felt strange against her skin after so long in linen, leather and wool. And yet, when she laced up the overdress, it felt as familiar as anything she'd worn at home. She looked down at the shimmery blue silk embroidered with gold thread, reminiscent of one of Queen Margareta's gowns. A wedding dress fit for a queen, or a princess. Too much for a mere lady, a girl who chased dragons and unicorns.

Melitta swallowed, then pushed open the door. George turned slowly, his eyes taking her in.

"My lady." He bowed so low, his head nearly touched the ground. "Never have I seen a woman more lovely."

She heard the clop of a horse's hooves, trotting across the bailey and out the gate. For good or ill, Princess Sativa had left in search of love, or her destiny.

Far more sensible than searching for dragons, Melitta now knew.

Her eyes met George's and they shared the same thought, though George's inability to read minds made him voice it.

"There was a drunk priest I passed on my

way here. If you are willing, Lady Melitta…" he began.

"A drunk priest, you say? Then I am more than willing," Melitta replied warmly, linking her arm through George's and leading him back to the feasting hall.

They paused outside so that George could help her cover her hair with the princess's veil. When he was satisfied that it was straight, they stepped into the hall together.

In almost no time at all, Melitta knelt beside George in the castle chapel, trying to make sense of the priest's words as he slurred through the ceremony.

King Boreslas and his court crowded into the room, talking so loudly they made it almost impossible to hear the priest.

"Melitta?" George prompted.

"Oh, yes, I do," Melitta replied.

More mumbling as the priest wrapped his stole around their joined hands, before he uttered something that ended with the word "wife".

Melitta rose, dusting off her knees. She had saved the hero from the princess, just like something in a fairytale.

"Godspeed, princess," she said softly.

"What?" George asked.

"Oh, nothing. Let's head for your bedchamber, before this drunken rabble decide to follow us," Melitta said. "I want you all to myself tonight."

George grinned. "I was thinking the same thing, my lady."

<h1 style="text-align:center">Forty-Three</h1>

Melitta was breathless by the time they reached George's chamber. She didn't want to let go of his hand, but she reluctantly did so when she realised he needed both hands to properly bar the door against intruders.

For a moment, George put his back to the door and just drank her in.

Being stared at so intently while she wore another woman's dress that Melitta knew was too long for her was disconcerting, to say the least. "I have chests full of dresses like this back in my mother's apartments. Ones that fit me far better, for Mother and I made them for me. Once we decide where we shall live, I can send for them. Or we could go fetch them…"

Her voice trailed off into silence as George stepped forward to claim a kiss. And another one. And she soon forgot everything about clothing until he said, "My lady, I confess that while you look beautiful in it, the only desire I have for your gown is to extract you from it."

She laughed, and helped him undo the lacings. His hands were so warm through the thin silk, it was almost like wearing nothing at all, until she found she really did wear nothing at all. She'd never been naked before a man before. Melitta folded her arms across her breasts, suddenly shy.

George was too busy shucking off his own clothes to notice. His surcoat, his tunic and even his hose lay on the flagstones, on top of the puddle of silk she'd shed.

His strong arms lifted her, carrying her to the bed. "I've dreamed of this," he said.

Melitta swallowed. "I know."

He laughed ruefully. "Of course. So you know that I am no expert at loving a woman but I would like you to enjoy it." He reddened.

So did Melitta. "I'm…I am no expert either, as you know this is my first time. But I have touched the minds of many couples when they…couple…and I think I know what I might like, or at least, what I would like to try."

At first, she guided his hands over her breasts and between her thighs, letting out little gasps of pleasure as with each touch, he awoke desires in her she'd never felt before. It was one thing to taste another's desire, but something else entirely to be devoured by her own.

She began to moan as George's fingers found a rhythm inside her that built and built and built to a climax that made her cry out.

When Melitta descended from on high, she knew only one thing: she wanted more. More of him, more of him inside her, and more of the pleasures only he could give her.

"My lady," he began, looking concerned.

Melitta pressed a finger to his lips. "I'm not your lady yet. First, you must fill me with more than your fingers, and then, when you are all mine, only then, will I be yours."

"As my lady wishes," he replied with a mischievous glint in his eye. He grasped her hips, spreading her thighs wide.

Melitta closed her eyes. This would hurt for only a moment, she knew, and then…

George's tongue darted inside her, licking and sucking at tender flesh until she cried out anew.

"George!"

Slowly, he withdrew, wiping his mouth with his hand. "When you are all mine, I want to hear you call me your lord."

Melitta inclined her head. "We have an accord."

Her mouth was dry in anticipation, but Melitta had no desire to drink. She wanted George, and if he was willing… "Will you…lie on your back? I would like to try…something."

Something that had made other women scream with pleasure. Something their lovers had enjoyed, too.

"As you desire, my lady." George flopped onto the furs, folding his arms behind his head.

Now she could truly take in the man she had married, in all his naked glory. Oh, she knew he was all lean, hard muscle, but one in particular drew her attention more than the others right now. She ran her fingers down his length, gently stroking him as she'd seen herself do in his dreams.

He groaned a little, thrusting his pelvis into her willing hands. She could give him pleasure with nothing but her hands, she knew, but neither of them would be satisfied with that. Not tonight.

Shivering in anticipation at her own daring, she climbed atop him. If she stroked him and he thrust his hips again in the same manner, he would be inside her.

Melitta made up her mind and reached

down.

George laughed and grasped her hips as he thrust upward without warning. The tiniest sting – a mere needleprick, healed in a moment – was over before it had barely begun, and she could think only of the heat of him, the hardness of his length as he drove into her. Slowly, masterfully, in control of every moment as he watched her reaction.

Melitta closed her eyes, lost in his love and the sheer sensation of making love – and being made love to – for the first time.

Steadily, another climax built within her as she felt the same need for release radiating from George. She knew he was close when he drove into her that penultimate time, sending her soul careening out among the stars. Yet she squeezed him within her, and felt his mind fly up alongside hers. The joint sensation was so exquisite, it surpassed anything she imagined even heaven could offer.

"Oh God!" she cried as George groaned his pleasure aloud.

Then she heard him laugh. "No, not a god. Just your lord, my lady. As you are mine."

She squeezed him again, and was surprised to discover it shot a little bolt of pleasure through her own loins. "My lord," she repeated. "I hope you plan on more lovemaking tonight, and every other night, because as long as you are my lord, I will want you in my bed."

She winced as George withdrew and went to clean himself up. "I will grant your wish, my lady, but I have one wish of my own."

"Oh?" Melitta tried to keep her face blank as the thought of all the things men liked their lovers to do in bed. She hoped he wasn't about to ask her to –

"In the interests of remaining your lord for as long as possible, I have one question about the dozen who died by your single blow."

Melitta swallowed. Oh. That.

"What did they do to offend you so, that they needed to die?"

She wet her lips. "They tried to steal my

honey from me."

His eyebrows flew up. "Honey? God forbid I ever try to steal your honey. I shall devote the rest of my life to providing you with every kind of sweetness you might desire, and defending you from anyone who might try to steal from you. May you never need to land another blow again."

It was her turn to laugh. "Not even if we hear of another dragon that must be slain?"

"Dragons are different." He lay down beside her once more. "And while I have never seen a lady look more beautiful in silk than you did tonight, I cannot get the vision out of my head of you, yesterday. Slaying that dragon and striding out of the flames like a goddess. Why, just the memory is enough to reinvigorate me for another round or two, at least."

"Another...?" Melitta followed his gaze and blushed. "I wanted to throw you down on the ground outside that cave and have my way with you," she admitted.

"Then you must have been reading my

mind."

He entered her again, chuckling at her gasp of delight, and between his tender lovemaking and passionate kisses, Melitta didn't care whether the thoughts in her head were his or her own. She loved him, and if he was the prize for slaying a dragon, the rest of the dragons in the world could go on living, for she had the most perfect happy ending to her very own fairytale, without a prince or princess in sight.

About the Author

Demelza Carlton has always loved the ocean, but on her first snorkelling trip she found she was afraid of fish.

She has since swum with sea lions, sharks and sea cucumbers and stood on spray drenched cliffs over a seething sea as a seven-metre cyclonic swell surged in, shattering a shipwreck below.

Demelza now lives in Perth, Western Australia, the shark attack capital of the world.

The *Ocean's Gift* series was her first foray into fiction, followed by her suspense thriller *Nightmares* trilogy. She swears the *Mel Goes to Hell* series ambushed her on a crowded train and wouldn't leave her alone.

Want to know more? You can follow Demelza on Facebook, Twitter, YouTube or her website, Demelza Carlton's Place at:

www.demelzacarlton.com

Books by Demelza Carlton

Ocean's Gift series

Ocean's Gift (#1)

Ocean's Infiltrator (#2)

Ocean's Depths (#3)

Water and Fire

Turbulence and Triumph series

Ocean's Justice (#1)

Ocean's Trial (#2)

Ocean's Triumph (#3)

Ocean's Ride (#4)

Ocean's Cage (#5)

Ocean's Birth (#6)

How To Catch Crabs

Nightmares Trilogy

Nightmares of Caitlin Lockyer (#1)

Necessary Evil of Nathan Miller (#2)

Afterlife of Alana Miller (#3)

Mel Goes to Hell series

Welcome to Hell (#1)

See You in Hell (#2)

Mel Goes to Hell (#3)

To Hell and Back (#4)

The Holiday From Hell (#5)

All Hell Breaks Loose (#6)

Romance Island Resort series

Maid for the Rock Star (#1)

The Rock Star's Email Order Bride (#2)

The Rock Star's Virginity (#3)

The Rock Star and the Billionaire (#4)

The Rock Star Wants A Wife (#5)

The Rock Star's Wedding (#6)

Maid for the South Pole (#7)

Jailbird Bride (#8)

The Complex series

Halcyon

Fishtail

Romance a Medieval Fairytale series

Enchant: Beauty and the Beast Retold

Dance: Cinderella Retold

Fly: Goose Girl Retold

Revel: Twelve Dancing Princesses Retold

Silence: Little Mermaid Retold

Awaken: Sleeping Beauty Retold

Embellish: Brave Little Tailor Retold

Appease: Princess and the Pea Retold

Blow: Three Little Pigs Retold

Return: Hansel and Gretel Retold

www.ingramcontent.com/pod-product-compliance
Lightning Source LLC
Chambersburg PA
CBHW070433120726
47910CB00003B/759